To Sam & Dean Winchester,
Thank you for 15 years.
I'll miss you idjits.

Chapter 1

RIVER

"I AM A FUCKING HERO."

I sit back with a satisfied grin, admiring my accomplishments.

Green M&M'S are superior, and that's why I've spent the last five minutes separating all of them from the rest.

My high lasts all of two seconds before I realize I'm out of things to do as I wait for my best friend, who is late for our Sunday morning coffee date again.

Blowing out an annoyed huff, I glance at the clock on the wall of the neighborhood's favorite diner. It only serves breakfast food and pie, which it's famous for.

This is my favorite place in the whole city.

The Gravy Train, an old train depot turned diner tucked in the middle of Harristown, Colorado. It's a small place, nothing fancy or extravagant inside, and it's home to not only the best breakfast around, but also the best pie. And I *love* pie.

They offer a few flavors a day, and my favorite—cherry—is available three times a week.

Sundays are cherry pie days.

A shuffle comes from the other end of the long stretch of

booth that takes up a sizeable amount of the back of the restaurant.

Lucy, a fellow regular here who also happens to be my apartment building manager, is up against the wall at the other end of the long community table where I like to sit. She's wearing a funky patterned poncho—a signature look for her—and her nose is stuck inside her crossword puzzle book. I've known her long enough to know that whenever her book is out, she's not coming up for air anytime soon.

"Seriously, River? Again?" Maya West, my best friend, stares down at me from the end of the table with a disappointed frown she's perfected over the years.

What did she expect me to do with my time? Sit here and twiddle my thumbs? I had to keep occupied somehow. She should know me better. I'm not the type to do something like pick up a newspaper or book for entertainment. Keeping my hands busy keeps my mind sane.

"What?" I pop a green candy into my mouth as she takes a seat. I wash it down with a big gulp of my now cooled coffee, which is loaded with enough sugar to put me in a coma. My pseudo-nephew, Sam, slides into the chair next to her. I stick my tongue out at my favorite little rascal, and he returns the gesture. I turn my attention back to Maya. "These precious babies don't belong with that"—I snarl my lip at the offending colors—"trash."

"They all taste the same," Maya argues, like she always does.

"Lies!" A few patrons inside scowl at my loud antics, but Sam laughs, which is what I'm truly aiming for. Now that he's twelve going on twenty, it's becoming harder to make him laugh as he transitions into his grumpy teenage years. I miss when all I had to do was cross my eyes at him and he'd giggle for five minutes straight.

"You're so strange." She scoots her chair closer to the table, tossing her long, chocolate hair behind her shoulder. "It's no wonder you can't find someone to date you."

Maya doesn't have a mean bone in her body, so her words aren't intended to sting, but they do.

Especially after yet *another* failed date last night.

My singlehood has been a bit of a daunting subject between us ever since I officially ended things with my ex.

We'd been together off and on for three years. Our relationship wasn't super serious and things had been stalling out for some time, and one day, I realized I was ready for more, something steady—and my ex wasn't. He was constantly flopping between jobs...and other people's couches, and I'm past that stage in my life. I knew I needed to cut my losses and move on.

I jumped back into the dating scene hard at first, going on a date a week at least. It didn't take long for me to realize what I was wanting—*stability*.

I'm not saying I'm ready for a trip down the aisle, but finding something...someone...that promises a future eventually would be nice.

After *a lot* of failed dates, I slowed it down. I've only been out with a handful of guys over the past year, all of them duds.

Maya thinks I'm being too picky, but I don't think there's anything wrong with knowing what you are (and aren't) willing to compromise on. Is it too much to ask that I find a guy who is funny, kind, has a steady job, *and* is hot?

It's not like I need to find *The One*, but consistent orgasms that don't come from my vibrator and someone to snuggle other than my cat Morris does sound nice, not to mention doing something other than working and hanging out with Maya and Sam—though I do love them dearly.

"I'm not strange," I tell her. "I'm...particular."

"You can say that again." She raises a brow, darting her eyes toward the pile of green M&M'S in front of me. "Speaking of dating, how'd last night go?"

I slide my eyes Sam's way, unsure if I want to spill the details of my latest dating misadventure in front of my godson. I'm sure he's not paying much attention, but it still feels weird considering I continue to see him as a toddler and not an almost teenager.

Maya notices my hesitation. "Hey, kiddo, go grab us some pie, would you? Cherry for your aunt River, of course." She digs around in her purse for far longer than is reasonable and finally thrusts her debit card into his hand. "And some coffee. You know what I like."

He grabs the card. "You should get a wallet, Mom. I don't think it's safe to leave your card loose in your purse like that."

"As opposed to leaving it in my wallet where a thief would *know* where it is?"

He rolls his eyes in response, and she grins in triumph.

"For the record," I say as Sam shuffles away, "I'm on his side with that."

"Says the girl who separates her M&M'S by color."

"The green ones are the best!"

"Remind me why we're friends again? We have zero in common."

"That's exactly why—it keeps things interesting. Plus, I

was the only person there for you during your whole pregnant-at-sixteen scandal."

She snorts out a laugh. "Right. That."

When I was eight, Maya's family moved in next door, and we became instant best friends. It didn't matter that we were total opposites and constantly fought over frivolous stuff like which boy band was better—we were inseparable.

We've been friends for twenty years now and have been through it all: high school drama, teenage pregnancy, marriage, becoming business partners, divorce...you name it. No matter what life throws at us, we're still thick as ever.

She's the sister I never had and always wanted.

"So, last night?" Maya purses her perfectly full lips, training her startling gray eyes on me.

"Right, right." I tap my chin. "Last night was...interesting."

"Good or bad?"

"Good...*ish*."

"You're doing a bang-up job clearing this up for me," Maya deadpans.

"Well, it started when my date—"

"Cheddar!" She claps her hands together, grinning like a fool. "Say it. Say his douchebag frat boy name that he is *way* too old to still be going by."

It *is* a ridiculous name. In fact, Cheddar might have been the first guy Maya didn't try to convince me to *give a shot*. I went out with him to prove I wasn't as picky as she claims.

My mistake.

"It started with *Cheddar* spilling his drink across the table."

"What was he drinking?"

9

"Why is that important?"

"A drink order says a lot about a person." Maya waves her hand impatiently. "Let's have it."

"Frozen strawberry daiquiri."

As soon as the words leave my mouth, I regret telling her.

She's laughing so hard she's not even making a sound as I sit there throwing daggers her way. I cross my arms over my chest, leaning back in my chair, letting her get it out.

"Are you finished yet?" She hasn't made a sound other than sucking in air for at least thirty seconds.

Finally, she expels a breath, wiping at her eyes. "Not only does he still go by *Cheddar*, he drinks *that*. I can't believe you didn't marry him on the spot."

"It was truly awkward when I ordered my whiskey neat."

"Attagirl."

I move on. "*Anyway*, the drink order and spill were something I could get over. Maybe he was nervous? Who knows? And when he mentioned still living with his mother? Whatever, the economy and all that. *But…*"

"Why do I have a feeling this is going to be good?"

"But then he said—and I fucking quote—that blackberry pie is the best kind of pie."

She clutches her chest. "He said what!"

I nod, puckering my lips. "I had the same reaction. In fact, I texted my mom and made her call me with an emergency to get out of there."

Maya rolls her eyes. "You realize I'm making fun of you, right?"

"What? You *know* cherry is the best kind of pie!"

"You can't keep pushing every Tom, Dick, and Harry

away for these asinine reasons. You'll never find anyone if you keep this up."

"First of all, I would *never* push a dick away."

"River..." Her voice is laced with frustration, and I get it.

I am kind of picky.

But is it too much to ask for a guy to make me...well, excited?

"Maybe I am a smidge particular, but nobody gets me going, you know? Nobody makes my heart rate spike or makes me laugh. Not one of them has been the sit-at-home-and-think-about-him kind of guy. Nobody has made me tingly in *all* the right places. Not a single date has—*ugh*."

In my peripheral, I watch the bane of my existence saunter through the doors of *my* favorite restaurant—which I've been frequenting for eight years now—like *he* owns the place.

His denim-clad legs stretch on for what seems like miles, and I don't even have to look to know he's wearing a t-shirt for some band that hasn't played a show in nearly thirty years. His coal black hair is messy like the wind blew it everywhere, and his face hasn't been shaved in three days.

He looks sloppy, like he just rolled out of bed and plucked his clothes from the floor. But, somehow, he's still ridiculously attractive...unfortunately.

"What? What's wrong?" Maya peers behind her to the front door of the diner, where my eyes have drifted. "Oh. Him."

"Yeah." I curl my lips back in disgust. "*Him.*"

She turns back to me. "I don't understand your problem with him. He's *super* hot."

"You don't live next door to him."

Not only does Lucifer himself patronize my favorite place

in the whole world, he also lives in the apartment right. Next. Door.

I see him all the time. At the mailboxes. In the elevator.

Every morning.

It's exhausting because *he's* exhausting.

Like the traitor she is, Maya lifts her hand and waves. He shoots her a grin I'm sure he thinks is panty-melting and waves back as he heads to the front counter to place his order.

I swat it down. "Stop that!"

"You stop it!" She yanks her hand back. "There's nothing wrong with him. He's—"

"*Super* hot—yeah, I heard you the first time. He's also *super* annoying."

"How so?"

"For starters, he—"

"Ah, Sam." My mortal enemy approaches the line. "Nice to see you, *bro*."

"That!" I practically rise up out of my chair, pointing an accusing finger at him. He peeks over at the commotion, thick brows squished together at my disruption. "That right there! He says stuff like that because—"

"Hey, Dean." Sam high-fives his old teacher. "How's your weekend going?"

"Because of that. They're Sam and Dean. Like *the Winchesters*." I roll my eyes. "Spare me," I finish as I settle back down on my ass, watching the two of them chat it up like old friends.

Which I guess they are. Kind of.

Last year when Maya and her ex were going through their divorce, Dean was there for Sam in ways only a father figure can be. With him being Sam's teacher and seeing him at school, the two grew close, and though it's incredibly silly, it makes me a little jealous.

And horny.

Which in turn makes me *really* damn angry.

I hate him. He's an ass. A total jerk. And *so* not my type. I don't like him. The attraction is the lack of a man warming my bed talking and nothing more.

Besides, what I'm looking for is *not* Dean. He might have a stable job and appear steady on his feet, but that doesn't make up for how much he annoys me.

"You know, I'm starting to think maybe you only say you hate him because you're secretly crushing on him."

I bark out a sardonic laugh. "Please. That is *so* not it."

"You're saying you don't find him attractive at all?"

"No."

"No you don't find him attractive, or no that's not what you're saying?"

I shift in my chair. "Of course I find him attractive."

"Huh. Interesting."

I tilt my head, pinching my brows together. "What is?"

"Dean turns you on."

"W-What?!" I sputter, sitting up straight. "He does not! Why would you say that? I never said that."

"You didn't have to. A best friend knows these things."

"What the…"

"Oh, honey." We look down the table toward Lucy, whose nose wasn't as stuck in her book as I thought. "It's obvious to me too."

"Lucy! What the hell?!"

She lifts a shoulder, a smirk teasing her red-painted lips. "I'm just tellin' the truth, dear. Besides, it ain't a bad thing.

You're not alone in your feelings—Dean makes me horny too."

My eyes widen and my cheeks heat.

"Now, now. Don't you two give me that look. I'm old, but there's still motion in this ocean, and the ocean is *definitely* in my panties when that man walks through the door."

She slides her tongue over her lips, and I have never wanted a hole to open up and swallow me as badly as I do in this moment, and that includes the time I walked through Wal-Mart with my skirt tucked into my underwear...my *thong* underwear.

Lucy takes a sip of her tea and turns her attention back to her book...*allegedly*.

Maya dips her head toward mine, leaning close to whisper, "So that happened."

"Unfortunately, it did."

"Look, it's not a bad thing if you have a crush on him."

"Just because he *might*—and I'm putting *a lot* of emphasis on that word—*maybe* get me a little excited in the pants, that doesn't mean it's a crush. I can be physically attracted to someone and still hate their guts."

"Or you can be lying."

I groan. "Trust me, it is *not* a crush, Maya. I don't even kind of like him. In fact, I've said many times over the last year that I *loathe* him."

"But for no good reason."

"You're kidding me, right? There are *plenty* of reasons!"

"Name one."

Just one? There are *so* many reasons to dislike Dean.

He's obnoxious. Always right about everything. Inserts

himself into breakfast with my best friend every single Sunday.

And his worst offense?

The fact that he lives next door. He's always playing that awful guitar on his balcony or blaring his horrid taste in music at all hours of the day. Screaming at the TV about whatever sport he always seems to be watching.

He's the worst neighbor ever.

"He wakes up to the same song every damn day."

"Most people do."

"But *Old Time Rock & Roll* repeatedly? It's—"

She points a finger at me. "That song is a classic. You're not allowed to trash-talk it."

"Classic or not, does he seriously have to blast that song at five thirty in the morning *including* weekends?"

"He works. That's more than I can say for half the dudes you go out on dates with."

"But—"

"No. No *buts*. Could he turn the music down? Sure, but you're not allowed to fault him for making a living, *especially* when it involves teaching and making kids' lives better."

"You're only saying that because he's all buddy-buddy with *your* kid."

"So?" She shrugs. "Now name something else that isn't absurd."

"Leo."

"Aw, come on. Leave Leo out of this."

I point to Dean, who's still standing in line with Sam because this place is packed on a Sunday morning. "I can't leave Leo out of this when he brought him here."

"Leo is *adorable*."

"He's a turtle!"

"But—"

"An emotional support turtle!"

"Yes, but—"

"In a damn restaurant!"

Maya huffs. "You're being a spoilsport."

I glance back at Dean, who is now engaged in conversation with another customer about said turtle. They're cooing at him like they would a baby. Leo's eating up the attention because he's as bad as his owner.

"He's only doing it for attention."

"Maybe the emotional support isn't for him but for Leo? Did you ever think about that?"

"Did you ever think that's the second most ludicrous thing to ever leave your facehole? Surpassed only by you telling me you can get Lyme disease by eating bad limes?"

"I saw it on Facebook!"

"Stay off Facebook!"

"But the drama...so addicting..." she murmurs. "Stop distracting me. We're talking about actual, viable reasons for hating him."

"He... He's..."

"What?" She sits forward, brows raised, waiting for my response. "Attractive? Funny? Friendly? Good with kids? Has a steady job?"

"He steals my pie!"

She rolls her eyes again. "He does not."

"Yes, he does. Intentionally. Every Sunday. It always happens."

"You're exaggerating."

"I am not."

"You sure about that?"

"I might be overstating it a bit, but you know I'm right about it happening often. We either get here too late and he's already snagged it because it's Sunday and the good pies always go fast on Sundays with people coming in and out after church taking them all—which is exactly why I want to meet early"—I give her a pointed look, and she shrugs sheepishly—"or he makes some futile excuse to trade whatever garbage he gets with Sam and your gullible little shithead buys it."

"One, you can order without me."

"I can't. Then it's not a true breakfast date. That's you running into me when I already have my face stuffed full of pie."

Ignoring me, she continues. "Two, there is no need for name-calling. Sam is not gullible."

"He's not? Because he believed he could get a fever from disco dancing on a Saturday night."

"He did not. Besides, he's just trying to be nice to his teacher—something you should be doing. Dean signed up to coach the football team this year, and your nephew likes football."

"Your point? Sam isn't my kid. I don't have to kiss Dean's ass for the sake of keeping the peace during the school year."

"Huh. And here I thought you *wanted* to kiss Dean's ass."

"What's that about my ass?"

Chapter 2

DEAN

IT NEVER FAILS.

Rain or shine, River White is always at The Gravy Train on Sunday mornings. Even if her best friend Maya doesn't show, River is here, because River loves cherry pie as much as I do.

Actually, I've concluded she likes anything sweet. She always seems to be snacking on green M&M'S, and because we've shared the same elevator on grocery days one too many times, I am aware of the things she buys, even when I don't want to be, like that time she bought a wholesale-sized box of condoms.

In the year I've lived here, I haven't met another person who annoys me and intrigues me as much as my neighbor does. One second, she's sweet and smiling. The next, she's ready to rip someone's head off.

Usually that someone is me.

If there's one thing about River I'm certain of—other than her love of pie—it's her hatred of me.

I let my eyes roam over her as she stares at me with a look that says, *I'll kill you, then I'll help them look for your body.*

Full of fire and probably a little bit of demonic possession, she stands just shy of five foot five. Her deep red hair—forged in the pits of hell, I'm sure—hangs loosely down her back, just begging to be pulled. Today she's wearing what I've come to recognize as her "I had another failed date and ate a pint of ice cream and half a box of cookies" attire: joggers and a shirt with more holes in it than Swiss cheese.

Yet, she's still drop-dead gorgeous.

And that's the part that irritates me the most.

No matter how often—and it's *very* often—River makes her feelings for me clear, I'm *still* undeniably physically attracted to her, even when I don't want to be.

She's borderline rude. She's obnoxious. Bossy. And she's the worst neighbor in the entire fucking world.

I only wish my dick would catch on to all that.

I plop down onto a stool across from my enemy.

"You were saying something about my ass?" I set my plate down and situate Leo on the table next to me. He ducks back into his shell, a little nervous of his surroundings, but he'll pop back out as soon as he sees there's no threat. For a creature that typically likes to do the solo thing, he's oddly friendly. Even more so on Sundays, the day I take him to the park and let him explore.

"Are you shitting me?"

River's angry mutter cuts through me…and heads south.

Like always, I ignore it.

There's no point in acknowledging it. I don't *actually* like her. It's my dick that likes her. It also likes when I see a shape in a wooden table that resembles a pussy.

It's nothing but my cock talking.

It's absolutely nothing personal and all just imagery.

"Come on now, River. I don't need to hear about your

shits. I'm trying to enjoy my pie." I stab my slice with my fork, shoving a healthy bite into my mouth.

She stares at me, lips twisted up with rage.

I grin at her around the delicious baked goodness.

Beats me why she despises me like she does, but I'd be lying if I said it wasn't fun to screw with her and get a rise.

She seethes, gritting her teeth. "I hate you."

"River!"

I swallow, wiping my mouth on my napkin. "It's fine, Maya. This isn't the first time River's made her feelings for me clear."

"You can say that again." Lucy, my building manager who totally loves me, backs me up without ever glancing away from her crossword book.

To my surprise, River's cheeks turn a deep red. I didn't think anything embarrassed her.

"Ignore my best friend."

Maya glares at River, who shrugs.

"I said what I said." She crosses her arms defiantly. "I hate him."

"She's just mad because I scored the last piece of cherry pie."

"Scored it? SCORED IT?" She inhales sharply. "You mean you swindled a gullible kid for it."

"Hey! I'm not gullible!"

"Oh, you're not?" River turns to Sam. "Then tell me what he told you to get you to switch a *cherry* slice for a *blackberry* one."

"He said he saw one of the servers touch it *after* she picked her nose. I didn't think you'd want to eat booger pie, Aunt River. I did it for you." He smiles proudly at himself.

Shit, this kid is too easy. I told him last week that it was illegal to eat cherry pie on that particular Sunday. He was scared River would get arrested and begged me to eat it myself.

Fool.

"You didn't think to question him when he then ordered booger pie for himself?"

I cut in. "I ordered everything at once. I didn't bring up the boogers until we were on our way over here with the goods."

"I have so many questions..." She narrows her eyes, trying to figure out where this is heading.

"Hit me with them. I'm a teacher—I get asked stupid questions all the time."

"You said there's no such thing as a stupid question." Sam tilts his head, staring at me accusingly.

"And I totally meant that for you, Sam. You never ask me stupid questions."

"Oh crap. My kid *is* gullible," Maya whispers, horrified.

I try not to laugh and give River my attention. "Well?"

"*You* paid for breakfast?"

"I always pay for breakfast."

"You do not! Maya and I rotate. One week it's me, then the next it's her. Always. We've never not done that. We..."

Her words die, and I'm sure it's because she's finally realizing that the mornings I'm here, there's never a charge on her card.

We might be enemies, but I was raised with manners.

Besides, I'm a little afraid my mom's My Kid is Being a Shithead senses would tingle, and she'd whoop my ass if I weren't doing the gentlemanly thing by paying for breakfast.

"You... You..."

"Me, me, what?" I mock. "Were you going to say I'm a kind, sweet, insanely attractive man? Because I know you weren't about to call me an ass."

I swipe an M&M from her stash and toss it into my mouth, grinning.

"You ass!"

"No." I push my finger against the table. "Nope. There are a few rules in life I abide by. If someone buys you pie, you absolutely can*not* call them an ass. Them's the rules, River."

She turns her nose up. "I don't care if you buy me pie. I still hate you."

"But a little bit less, right?"

She doesn't say anything, but I can see it in her eyes.

They shift down to Leo, then roll right back in her head.

"Hey, be nice to Leo. He doesn't deserve your wrath."

"Seriously? You brought your turtle—I'm sorry, *emotional support turtle*—to breakfast. Again. What the hell?"

She can be mean to me all she wants, but Leo? No way. The little fella has been through the wringer.

"Listen, Ms. Sasshole. Leo isn't *my* emotional support turtle. *I'm* his emotional support handler. He was injured when he lived with his last owner. I'm helping nurse him back to health."

Her eyes widen with surprise.

Yeah, River, I'm not a total asshole. Sure, I might blare my music and steal your pie, but I do have a heart.

She shakes her head. "You're making that up."

I lean into the table. "Am not."

"Are too," she argues, matching my movements.

I shift another inch.

22

So does she.

Hazel.

Her eyes are hazel.

I don't know why I'm only now noticing—probably because this is the closest I've ever been to her—but her eyes are the most beautiful combination of gold and green I've ever seen.

Her tongue peeks out and slides across her lips, and I track the movement.

I can't look away because *fuck me* her mouth is so damn kissable, and it's been entirely too long since I've kissed somebody.

It lasts so long that I'm sitting here contemplating closing the distance between us like this isn't River fucking White across from me. Like she doesn't hate me. Like I don't hate her.

"Am not," I force myself to say instead.

"Are—"

"You know, dears, if you wanted your own private space, we could all leave," Lucy interrupts.

We jump apart like we've been caught doing something we shouldn't, and Leo darts back into his shell, startled by the sudden movement.

"Sorry, buddy." I run my finger down the plastic hut, trying to soothe him.

And myself a bit.

River's hot and gets my dick going, but kissing her? Hell would have to freeze over first.

The attraction is there, but she's my neighbor who is constantly trying to ruin the best apartment I've ever had by making complaints and annoying me. I love my place way too much to start dating my neighbor, let things get all screwed up, and have to move…again.

I will never, *ever* kiss River White.

That I can promise.

"I'm going pee." River shoots off her stool and practically runs to the bathroom.

She's annoyed with me for buying her breakfast.

Good. Maybe she'll think twice before she glares at me again for breathing too loudly for her liking.

"If that doesn't make the guys hot, I don't know what will." Maya shakes her head at her friend's retreating back.

"She sure is something else." I take another bite of my cherry pie, which, sadly, is almost gone.

Was it a little petty of me to convince Sam to give me the last slice of cherry? Sure.

Do I regret it? Not one damn bit.

She's the one who started this war between us, reporting me to Lucy with senseless noise complaints a week after I moved in instead of coming over and asking me to turn it down. I was willing to let us have a clean slate after the thing with her cat, but not her, apparently.

Besides, I don't turn my shit up *that* loud. There was no need to go to Lucy with that trivial crap like she's done four times now.

Luckily, Lucy takes pity on me—I'm ninety-nine percent certain she's crushing on me—and doesn't take the accusations any further than giving me a not-so-stern warning.

I'll stop being petty once River does.

"So, Dean, are you looking forward to summer school starting in a couple weeks? Are you excited to start coaching football?"

Nodding, I swallow and take a sip of my coffee. "Very much so, to both. The only part I like about summer is getting to spend more time with Leo. I'd much rather be in the classroom."

It's true, too.

I love teaching. I love the kids and the wild shit they say. I love seeing the expressions on their faces when something clicks in their mind.

And coaching? Man, I can't wait to start. When the team's old assistant coach moved away at the end of the school year, I was first in line to apply for the spot. I loved playing football in high school and college. I knew I was never good enough to go pro, but that didn't change how much I loved the game.

I'm looking forward to spreading my love of the sport.

"Sam, you're trying out, right?"

He peeks up from his phone. "I'm not sure," he mutters, eyes flitting over toward his mother, the worry in them clear as day. "I, uh, I don't know if I can."

I don't miss the way Maya's smile wavers.

I've seen Maya around on the weekends enough to know she's been struggling since her divorce, putting in extra hours at work while still trying to be there for her son, and I'm sure it's draining on her. Football is a pricey sport to get into, and I'm sure she's worried about the financial aspects as much as she is about the time commitment.

"I told you, we'll make it work," she tells him.

"But your work schedule…"

"Don't worry about my work schedule. Besides, Aunt River can help get you to and from games and practices. It'll all be fine." She winks at her son. "Pinky promise, kiddo."

Great. Because more River is just what I need in my life.

He rolls his eyes. "Mom, I'm too old for pinky promises."

"Dude, you are *never* too old for pinky promises. They're a binding contract no matter your age."

He shrugs, shoving his face back in his phone and getting lost in whatever is on the screen.

"Kids." Maya huffs.

I chuckle. "You're preaching to the choir."

"I don't know how you do it. A classroom full of them..." She shakes her head. "I can barely handle the one I have."

"To be fair, I get to go home at night and have a kid-free evening where I blast my music or play my guitar. I get a break, you don't. That's the difference."

"Speaking of your evenings...you know you're driving River nuts with that, right?"

I smirk. "Oh, I'm aware."

She laughs at my lack of remorse. "Why do you insist on torturing my best friend?"

Just then, River comes waltzing out of the bathroom. I'm unable to stop myself from admiring the way she carries herself with confidence, even in her hideous joggers and raggedy shirt. She's virtually dressed like a hobo and my dick *still* isn't getting the memo that there's nothing good that can ever come from getting excited about her.

Maya clears her throat, drawing my attention.

I peel my eyes away from River, doing my best to look like I wasn't lusting after her best friend.

"Because she insists on torturing me."

She quirks a brow, and I can see the questions forming on her lips.

"You're still here?" River complains, unknowingly saving me from whatever Maya was about to ask. *Thank fuck.* She slides back onto her stool, glaring at me. "I thought if I took long enough, you'd be gone."

"Leave without saying goodbye to my favorite nemesis? I don't think so. Besides, I'm not done with my *delicious* cherry pie yet. It's so warm, so sticky sweet...*so* perfect."

Her nostrils flare as I slide a bite into my mouth.

"Mmm," I moan. "So good."

"Hate. You."

"You wish you did."

"What's that supposed to mean?"

"Come on, River. You're obviously fixated on me."

She curls her lip. "You're disgusting."

"Or I'm right."

She blows out an exasperated breath. "And on that note, I'm leaving."

"What? Why?" Maya sticks her bottom lip out in a pout.

"Aw, so soon?" I tease.

Her icy eyes land on me as she gathers her things. "Yeah, I want to stop by the shop before Caroline opens to check up on a few things. We could have had more time together if someone wasn't late..."

"Blame your nephew." Maya hitches a thumb toward her son. "It was his fault."

"It's *always* his fault."

She shrugs. "Guess someone needs to get a better handle on him, then."

"That's *your* job."

"Ugh, don't remind me." She stands and wraps her arms around River, pressing a kiss to her cheek. "You don't need to work all the time, River. We're all in this business together now. Take a day off."

Not that I give a shit about what River does, because that would imply thinking about her in any capacity outside of her annoying me, but Maya's right.

River *is* always working. It's a miracle she even finds time to complain to the building manager about me—she's hardly ever home.

"I know, I know. It's my baby though. You have your kiddo to take care of, and I have mine. Besides, I could use some getting out of the apartment and not dwelling on my horrid love life."

"I'll give you that, but promise me it'll be a quick in and out. Deal?"

"Deal." River returns the hug. "Love you. I'll call you later." She ruffles Sam's messy hair, which is the exact shade of his mother's. "Later, kiddo. I'm picking you up for ice cream tomorrow morning, right?"

"Ice cream in the morning?"

"You're one to talk." She drops her eyes to the empty plate in front of me. "You just ate cherry pie for breakfast."

"It has fruit in it…"

"Fine. I'll make sure they throw a couple strawberries on his ice cream." She tosses a wink at him like I can't see her. "Extra strawberries—Mr. Evans said so."

Sam scrunches his nose up. "Can you not?"

"Bye, Lucy." River sends her a wave.

"Have a good day, love. Your secret's safe with me." She winks, and River's cheeks heat again as her eyes dart my way.

"What secret?" I ask.

"It's nothing," Maya says, attempting to cover for her friend.

"Oh, it's not nothing. It's a disgusting notion that I'm

secretly crushing on you, which is damn absurd if you ask me. It's perfectly clear I hate your guts."

Lucy thinks River is crushing on me?

Interesting...

"Isn't that ridiculous?" She rolls her eyes. "You? Please. You would be so lucky."

My lips twitch at her confidence. She's so sure of herself.

"I don't think lucky is the word you're looking for here."

"Oh, trust me. It is."

I snort, pushing back from my stool, stacking the plates together, and balancing them on top of Leo's hut. I nod toward Maya and Sam. "See you guys next week." I stop shoulder to shoulder with River and bend until my mouth is hovering at her ear. "Trust me. It isn't. And don't worry, your secret crush is safe with me."

She cranes her neck to look up at me, her green and brown orbs full of ire.

I smirk. "Later, River."

Chapter 3

RIVER

"ASININE, asshole jerkface. *Trust me. It isn't.* Ugh. Whatever. You can shove your sexy-as-sin smirk right up your—"

"Um, River? Are you okay?"

I glance up, stopping in my tracks in the doorway of Making Waves, the boutique I've worked my ass off to make a hit.

"You good, boss?" Caroline's baby blue eyes are filled with concern as she gives me a small smile.

I sigh. "Yeah, I'm fine. It's just…"

"Dean again?" She grins knowingly.

"He's the worst."

"That's what I hear." She grabs another set of earrings, setting them in the display case. "Though I'm not sure how someone with a voice like that can be the worst."

"That is my exact issue—*you* can hear him from two stories down."

She laughs, shaking her head. "Yes, but I'm not complaining about it. Cooper doesn't complain either. That makes it two against one, not including the rest of the tenants who stand on their balconies, cheering him on…"

"But you're not *right next door* to him. It's different."

30

"I'm sure it is," she murmurs, finishing organizing the first jewelry station and moving on to the next.

I ignore the way she says it, like there's more she's hinting at.

"How did closing go last night?" I slide behind the counter, logging on to the computer to check up on things.

"We had someone come in thirty minutes before close, and she ended up buying five pieces. Gave us the best day of the month."

Relief zings through me.

I started Making Waves on my own five years ago. Despite the way I'm currently dressed, I've always loved clothes and accessories. Finding the right outfit and shoes can change my whole mood—something I should have considered when I woke up crabby—and I love helping others find a piece that makes them feel good too.

When I graduated college with a BA in business management, I knew I wanted to make those four grueling years worth it by doing something I enjoy.

Starting a company on my own wasn't easy. At times, it downright sucked. Business was slow, almost nonexistent in the beginning. For the first three years, it was just me. I couldn't afford to hire anyone else. I'd have been dead on my feet in the first six months if it weren't for Maya volunteering all her time to help me keep the fledgling business alive.

One month, business *finally* picked up. Then it happened again. And again. The trend continued to tick upward, and I was so swamped I *had* to officially hire someone or I'd have burned myself out completely.

Caroline stumbled through the door looking for a job at just the right time two years ago. With Maya *finally* divorcing her asshole ex and needing a job ASAP, I knew she'd make the perfect addition to the business too.

There was a lot of sweat and tears, but the three of us continued our upward trend in sales, even expanding to having a mobile shop for pop-up events, and earlier this year, we dipped our toes into online.

Though there are plenty of days where I feel like it will all be ripped away at a moment's notice, it's starting to feel like I'm actually going to make it. Knowing what our previous best day this month was and exceeding it…well, it totally makes up for Dean stealing my pie this morning and firmly puts me in a good mood.

"Good. That's good."

"Breathe, River. You look like you're carrying the weight of the world on your shoulders. We're doing good—*better* than good. You can relax a little, you know."

I throw a glance her way over the top of the computer screen. "You sound like Maya."

"Don't tell her I said this, because she'd never stop gabbing about it, but she's right."

I grab my phone and hold it up. "Can you repeat that? I need to get it on record for blackmail later."

"I'll take it to my grave, thank you." She pushes my hand away. "But I'm serious, boss."

"I heard you," I mutter. "That's a cute top. One of yours?" I ask to distract her, and because it *is* a cute top.

In fact, her whole outfit is pretty. Her long legs look amazing in a pair of simple skinny jeans that are fringed at the bottom, leading to a pair of plain white shoes. The real star of the show is her oversized pattern-blocked top that hangs off one of her shoulders. It's trendy and fun.

She looks so put together, unlike me.

Whatever. It was a long, rough night, and not in the way I wanted it to be.

I'm almost starting to think Maya might be onto something about me being picky...

Caroline's cheeks redden at the subject change. She revealed her secret talent for designing clothes about six months ago. I've been begging her to make a few pieces for the shop, but she's painfully shy about it. Well, that and everything else it seems.

Though her bashfulness has improved since she moved here, there are still some things she's tight-lipped about, her design abilities being one of them.

The only person I've seen her flourish around is her childhood best friend and roommate, Cooper. She insists they're just friends, but I swear there's something brewing between them. I have never seen two people so in tune with one another before, but I guess the same could be said about Maya and me, and I can confirm there's nothing brewing between us.

It's just my romance-deprived mind trying to find something that isn't there.

She tucks away one of the tendrils hanging free from the long dark blonde hair that's piled in a messy bun on the top of her head. "It is."

"It would—"

"Look lovely in the front window?" She smirks. "I know, and I love you for saying that. I'm just not ready."

I laugh. "Am I that predictable?"

"Yes, just like I know you're about to say *When you are ready, you know I'm here.* Like you always do."

33

"But—"

"River…"

"Okay, okay." I hold my hands up. "I won't say anything else."

"Good. Now, what are you doing here?" Caroline checks the watch on her wrist, then pushes off the counter, heading toward the front door. "Today is your day off."

"Just checking in on things." I don't mention to her that I was also here earlier this morning working on inventory when I was unable to sleep and going mad inside my apartment.

"Do you not trust me?"

"Of course I trust you. I—"

"Did some big order come up?"

"No. I—"

"Did you *need* to come in?"

"Well, no. But—"

"Then go home, River." She flips the open sign on and straightens a mannequin's blouse before making her way back over to the counter. "There's no reason for you to be here. You're here so much I'm starting to think you have a cot in the back office. I mean, you *do* look like you might have slept here…"

I let out a long, tired groan, rubbing at my eyes. "Gee, thanks."

"Was your Cheeseman date so bad you couldn't sleep?"

"His name was *Cheddar*, Caroline. Cheddar! Of *course* the date was that bad."

"Sorry." She winces. "Maybe you should take a break. All these failed dates are wearing you out. I mean…" She darts her eyes to my outfit.

I sigh defeatedly. "You might be right."

She pulls her phone from her pocket, holding it out to me. "Can you repeat that? Gonna need it for blackmail later."

I roll my eyes. "Remind me again why I hired you?"

"Because I was the only person desperate for the paltry salary you were offering? Which reminds me…you are paying *me* to be here today, not yourself. So…"

I lift a brow. "Your subtlety needs work."

"Oh, I wasn't trying to be subtle, River. You need a break from this place. Take *at least* one night off. It won't kill you."

"How do you know? It could. I've never tried, and I'm still alive. Why risk it now?"

"*That* is the exact problem—you've never tried. Everything is fine here. Go home."

I groan. "All right. I'll leave."

"And go home, where you'll stay the entire night," she instructs. When I open my mouth, she shakes her head and points a finger at me. "Nope. I don't want to hear it. No calling either."

I smash my lips together, nodding, accepting my fate. I grab my purse, rounding the counter.

"Home and no calling," I promise.

"Good." She grabs me by the shoulders, ushering me toward the shop door. "Take a bath or something. You need to relax."

Oh, man. A bath. Water so hot I can barely stand it. Candles and a good book. That sounds like heaven… "A bath does sound good."

"Have a whiskey in there. Or cake. Eating cake in the bathtub *always* makes me feel better."

"Cake in the tub? But pie…"

"Then get pie. Do it. Trust me."

"Whatever you say." I wrap my arms around her, squeezing her tight. "Thank you, Caroline. I don't know what I'd do without you sometimes. I'm so happy you said yes to the paltry salary."

She laughs, hugging me back. "Me too. Now go home."

"I thought I was the boss around here…"

"Not today. I'll call you tomorrow." She practically shoves me out the door, clicking the lock shut behind me.

"You better remember to unlock that!"

She rolls her eyes, waving me off.

I take a deep breath and turn toward my apartment building, which is five blocks away.

Home. A nice bath. A glass of whiskey.

They're all calling my name.

First stop, pie.

"MORRIS! GET DOWN FROM THERE!"

Meow.

"Yes."

Meow.

"I am your treat-giver. You better listen to me, mister."

Meow.

"Dammit, Morris! You're going to fall in and go nuts and ruin this whole experience for me."

This is what my life has come to—arguing with my cat while I take a bath, slice of pie in hand.

The little shit finally hops down, only to jump onto the toilet and into his favorite spot in the apartment: the bathroom sink.

He meows again.

"Good. I'm glad you found your spot. Now let me relax in peace. Swear, I am never having kids," I mutter. "If a cat is this demanding, hard pass on children."

I scoot down in the tub, careful to keep my pie safely above water.

When I was first looking at apartments, number one on my must-haves list was a big bathtub. It might seem like a trivial requirement, but nothing beats a good soak when the demons living in my uterus try to murder me once a month.

Or when I need to unwind.

Like today.

I stab at my slice of Dutch apple from The Gravy Train, my second favorite thing they serve. I moan when the flavor hits my tongue and sink lower into the tub, the hot water already working its magic on the tension that's beginning to feel permanent.

Maya and Caroline are right—I *do* work too much. Just this week, I put in over fifty hours at Making Waves. It's not the first time I've done it this month either. Overloading on work is a flaw of mine, a tactic I use to avoid everything else I don't want to think about.

This is why I've officially reached a new low by eating pie and drinking whiskey in the damn tub at two in the afternoon.

I'm overworked and undersexed.

I could have fixed that sex thing last night with my date, but there was no way I was letting him take me home.

Cheddar. Ugh. Such a laughable name. I shouldn't have tried to prove Maya wrong and go on the date to spite her because he was *awful*—and not just because of his (lack of) taste in pie.

I've never met a more boring person in my entire life.

I thought maybe he'd have a good story about his obtuse nickname, but it was nothing more than him refusing to eat any kind of cheese other than cheddar and his college roommates picking on him for it.

That was the grand story he took fifteen minutes to tell me as we waited for our table because he made the reservation for later than we agreed upon. His reasoning was, *"You know... because women."*

His misogynistic remark coupled with him being more boring than watching paint dry let me know right then I wasn't going on another date with him.

That was when I texted my mom to get me out of there.

I barely even waited until we were at a table—the one he spilled his frozen drink all over.

Ugh.

Okay, so maybe I *do* make rash decisions to ditch on these dates, but at least I am aware of what I will and won't settle for.

I take another bite of apple pie, trying to make myself feel better about my inability to find a normal guy to date.

Maybe I *should* just give up.

I have good friends. My business is thriving. I'm happy with where I'm at most days. There's no reason to rock the boat...but man do I wish someone would rock *my* boat.

"Stop whining about your pitiful sex life, River. You're supposed to be relaxing, not bitching and moaning. This is a time of calm, of peace. Chill. Re—"

"STILL LIKE THAT OLD TIME ROCK 'N' ROLL!"

"Oh, sweet Jesus!"

I jump, and my precious slice of apple pie goes flying.

And lands right in my bathwater.

"Are you serious?!" I scream, glaring at the wall that's vibrating from the awful music thumping in the apartment next to mine.

Dean...again!

This is the same thing that happened last time I took a bath—he ruined it like he ruins everything else good in my life. I bet I'd be ten times more relaxed if I didn't have *him* as a neighbor.

I'm over it. Completely fed up.

I shove up out of the tub, water sloshing over the sides, but I don't care.

I'm pissed.

Furious.

Abso-fucking-lutely *done* with Dean Evans.

Chapter 4

DEAN

"DO you want to hear what shit your mother is trying to pull now?"

"I need a damn beer for this," I mumble as I push my key into the slot and unlock my apartment door.

I don't care that it's only two in the afternoon; the tone in my little sister's voice reeks of exasperation, and I know I'm about to hear some shit.

"Tell me when you're ready." I hear her take a gulp out of what I can only assume is an afternoon wine because I know my sister.

"It's sad we're both already drinking this early."

"Hey! I'm at brunch. It's okay to day-drink if you call it brunch."

"Is two in the afternoon still brunch?"

"If it allows me to day-drink mimosas, then yes." I picture her smirking victoriously. "Are you ready for this yet?"

"Let me get Leo back in his terrarium first." I balance the phone between my ear and shoulder as I set him down on the countertop, popping the latches on his on-the-go hut. "We just got back from the park."

"Aw, how is my little buddy?"

"He's Leo—a little shithead."

"How can a *turtle* be a shithead?"

"Trust me on this, Holland." I pick him up and settle him in his home. "He's mischievous as hell."

"You don't sound eccentric at all, Dean."

"Well, shit. I feel *so much* better hearing that from you."

"I am *not* eccentric."

"You do have like four cats…" I make my way to the kitchen, using my elbow to turn on the water. I use the same elbow to pump soap into my hands and wash up like I'm getting ready for surgery. Ain't no salmonella going to get me.

"They're foster cats, you…you…butthole!"

"The fifth graders I teach have better comebacks than that."

"That's because they're all young and hip. I'm old and not hip."

I laugh, turning off the water and grabbing the dishtowel hanging off the edge of the sink to dry my hands. "Nobody says hip anymore, Holland."

"Which proves my point."

"You're younger than me."

"By fifteen months! That doesn't count."

"It counts, little sis." I grab the phone with my hand again and stretch out the kink forming in my neck. I peel open the fridge and pluck out a beer.

"Are those bottles I hear clinking?"

"Those are my brunch beers, yes." I hold the bottle up to the opener I have sticking to the fridge. "And this is a brunch beer bottle opening." I pop the top and instantly take a hefty swig. Leaning my back against the counter, I cross one leg over the other. "All right, kiddo, let's hear it. What did your mom do now?"

"Do you remember Brett Johnson from high school?"

"That guy who found a way to bring up his stepmom in *every* conversation and it started becoming way too creepy? Unfortunately, yes."

"Beyond creepy. I just got done having my weekly face-to-face with Mom, and guess who she set me up with?"

"Gross. Why?"

"Because she hates me, that's why."

"Mom doesn't *hate* you. It's just obvious *I'm* her favorite."

My sister laughs lightly, but I know that bit of knowledge hurts because it hurts me too.

Our parents didn't get the whole "you're not supposed to pick favorites" memo.

I'm Mom's favorite, and Holland is *definitely* Dad's.

We picked up on it early and settled into the reality, promising each other to never let it come between us. Unlike a lot of siblings, Holland and I get along like two peas in a pod. We didn't have a choice but to lean on each other growing up in our house. It always felt like our parents were more divorced than they were married. It was awkward to navigate, and their favoritism didn't do anything to help ease the tensions.

Still, we never let them affect our sibling relationship. Aside from my childhood friend Nolan—and I guess Leo, though I'd never tell her that—she's my best friend.

"Are you going to go out with him?"

"Do I have a choice?" She groans. "You know your

mother will guilt me into it either way. At least she didn't set me up with Sutton Barnes," she grumbles.

Even though we've been doing it for years, I still grin when she calls Mom *my* mother.

"Unless..." Holland's taking the conversation exactly where I thought she would.

"Ah, so *that's* why you called—to get me to convince Mom to let you out of this date."

"And because you're my favorite brother."

"Uh-huh." I take another long pull from my beer.

"Please, Dean? Pretty, *pretty* please? I don't want to go on this date because I'm like ninety-nine percent certain this guy is boning his stepmom. Why Mom would set me up with him is beyond me."

"Hello, his last name is Johnson. You know his bank account is large, and Mom's kind of...well..."

"Materialistic? Always looking for a way to climb the social ladder even if it means putting her children in harm's way? A monster?"

"Holland..."

"What? You know I'm not wrong, Dean."

The sad part is, she's right. Our parents aren't awful people. They're just...misguided by money.

When I was thirteen, we hit the jackpot. My dad won the *actual* lottery, and he took the payout of about one hundred and fifty million. A lot of money to almost anyone, but it was especially a lot of money to us, a family of four living meager paycheck to meager paycheck. We didn't live in The Heights —the neighborhood that seemed to sprout nothing but criminals—like Nolan did, but we were right on the line.

The money came at just the right time, and Dad was smart

with his winnings. He set aside enough for college for both me and Holland, then invested the rest into a business idea he had been cooking up for years.

It worked, and in the first year, he made back twice as much as what he had invested.

Before we knew it, we were moving and starting school in the rich part of town.

"I mean, yeah, you're kind of right," I agree. "Except for the monster part. Mom's not out to get you. She's just—"

"Sticking her nose where it doesn't belong? Like in my dating life?"

I chuckle. "Yes, that. If it makes you feel any better, she does it to me too."

"And look how that turned out for you!"

She means my last relationship, which ended in disaster and me moving to a different city.

Holland clears her throat. "Sorry. I shouldn't have said that. But...does this mean you'll help me get out of it?"

Do I want my sister dating some dude who's clearly hung up on his stepmom? No.

Am I going to bend over backward to get her out of this date? Also no.

But I'll talk to our mom and try to get her to budge. Holland has enough on her plate with our father ruling her life. She doesn't need to add my mother's meddling to the mix.

"I'll see what I can do. You could always just not go, you know."

"And disappoint your mother again? Since she's *still* pissed at me after our last blowout, I don't think so."

"I can't imagine being on Mom's bad side is any worse than being on Dad's shitlist."

Which is exactly where I am and have been for the last... well, forever, it feels like.

"I wouldn't know—I've never been there."

"Must be nice." I push off the counter and drop my empty beer bottle into the recycling bin. "Speaking of Dad...when are you going to ask him about the promotion?"

"Um...never. He'll never go for it."

"You never know. Doesn't hurt to try. Besides, it'd be nice. You could move out here and get away from that town, Holland. It's no good. Sucks you in, chews you up, and spits you out all wrong."

"You know when you say things like that, you imply *our parents* are no good, right?"

"Mom *is* meddling in your dating life when you're nearly thirty."

"Dean..." Her tone tells me to drop it.

It's the same old fight we've been having for years now. I was smart enough to get away while I still could, but not Holland. My dad has her under his control because she feels indebted to him for some reason. It's why she still lives in that asshole-infested community and why she's still working as his secretary, even though she deserves a better position at the company.

Since I don't feel like arguing today, I redirect the conversation. "When's your date?"

"Friday night."

"Look, I'll call Mom tonight and see if I can start sweet-talking her into canceling it."

She squeals loudly into the phone. "Thank you, thank you, thank you. You're the best big brother a girl could ask for."

"Remember that next time I need something."

"Please, you know I always have your back, Deanie Weenie," she teases.

I groan at the use of the nickname I hate.

"*Now* you're pushing your luck."

"You're just mad because you don't have a nickname to torture me with."

True. "Whatever. Look, I'm gonna go. Need to shower. I'm all gross from being at the park, and I need to make some lunch. The pie I had this morning just isn't cutting it."

"Pie for breakfast again?"

"Says the girl drinking orange juice and champagne."

"Mimosas are totally a breakfast food! Pie isn't."

"Then why does The Gravy Train sell it at breakfast?" I retort.

"First of all, that name is utterly ridiculous, and you know it. Second…you went to the diner for breakfast, didn't you? Please tell me you did not torture your neighbor *again*."

I grin. "I didn't torture my neighbor again."

"Liar! You should be nice to her, Dean. She's a sweet gal."

"How do you know? You've never met her."

"She's lived next door to you and your antics for the last year and still hasn't murdered you. That's a huge indication that she's way too nice."

I try not to roll my eyes over the fact that yet another person—my own sister, no less—is taking River's side.

Did they ever stop to think that I torture River because she's mean to me for no damn reason?

Sure, I'm probably way too old to be acting this juvenile,

but she brings it out in me. River's wound too tight. She needs to learn to relax and stop taking everything so seriously. She's wearing herself down and taking it out on everyone else.

"I'll take that into consideration next time I'm cooking up some revenge."

Holland doesn't bother hiding her tired sigh. "You're something else, big brother."

"Don't I know it, little sister. Love you, kiddo."

"Love you too...Deanie Weenie!"

The line goes dead.

Brat.

After a quick rinse in the shower, I'm back in the kitchen pulling out the fixings for a hearty grilled turkey, bacon, and cheese sandwich. I grab the skillet from the cabinet beside the stove and crank the heat. I need this baby to warm up pronto. I am famished.

"Counter robot!" I command my smart device. "Play my Morning Music playlist."

Bob Seger's *Old Time Rock & Roll* hums quietly through the apartment, and my mood instantly lifts.

I pull out two pieces of sourdough and slather butter on each one. I load the bread up with turkey and cheese then hold my hand over the pan, seeing if it's ready for the bacon.

"Come on, pan. You know I'm starving." I shake my head when I realize I'm talking to an inanimate object. "I might be going mad. I should get another beer."

I grab another from the fridge and pop the top. I don't normally drink this early in the day, but today I'm saying fuck it.

It's probably just the heat making me feel so worn out, but this day feels like it's about ten years long.

47

Or it could be talking to my sister. Or dealing with River this morning.

She always has that effect on me.

When the pan is finally ready, I slap a few slices of bacon in there and let them do their thing. The fat begins to sizzle, and the smell makes my stomach growl.

I swivel around to the sink and turn the water on to start rinsing off the knife and wiping down the sink. I learned early on when I started living on my own that if I don't clean as I go when in the kitchen, it'll never get done.

I'm not a slob, but I could use improvement in a few areas. I try to keep a clean apartment in case my mother decides to do one of her surprise visits—like she did last week when she ripped into me for having a pizza box on the living room table.

"...soothes my soul," I sing quietly as I clean. "I reminisce—Man, Leo, I don't think I'll ever get tired of this song. It's a damn classic, isn't it?"

He doesn't respond.

Not because he isn't listening, but because he's a turtle.

If there's one thing I can count on Leo for, it's listening.

Or at least that's what I tell myself when I'm talking to him alone inside my apartment like a nutjob.

Being alone doesn't bother me. I prefer it, really. That's why I did everything I could to get away as fast as possible. Well, that and the people—the rich pricks who run the place and coast on Mommy and Daddy's money.

The private school my parents sent us to after we hit the jackpot wasn't my thing. The students were all elitist assholes, and all the teachers did was kiss their asses.

At the end of it all, I suppose I should thank them. They're a big reason I wanted to become a teacher. If I can save a couple kids from feeling as misplaced as I did, I'll be happy.

And that's what I am: happy.

I crank up my smart device, letting the tunes wash over me, and take a healthy pull from my beer.

"Ahh, much better."

I smack my lips together, then check the bacon. It's almost done. Just a few minutes and then I can put the rest of my lunch together and be on my way to sandwich heaven.

I grab the dishtowel to busy myself and start wiping away the breadcrumbs from next to the stove.

BANG, BANG, BANG!

Several harsh blows land on my front door.

"What the…"

I toss the cloth toward the counter and pad to the entryway.

I put my eye up to the peephole, but whoever is out there is covering it.

That can only mean one thing…

"What the fuck, River?" I yank the door open. "Why are you banging on my door like you're the cops. I'm—"

My words die on my tongue when I get a look at her.

River White is standing before me in nothing but a towel.

A *small* towel.

Like so tiny I'm certain if she were to bend over, I would see *everything*.

And damn do I want to make her bend over.

Her short legs look long in the scrap of material, and it hugs all her curves, leaving nothing to the imagination. The long red hair that's usually hanging down her back is swept up in a clip. Her skin is dewy, like she's just gotten out of the shower and didn't properly dry off.

Shit. Now I'm imagining River in the shower...

"Seriously?" Her wintry tone drags me from my fantasy.

She crosses her arms over her ample chest, the petite towel rising with the movement. Her hazel eyes are trained on me, formed into thin slits.

River isn't here to show me how sexy she looks in next to nothing.

She's pissed and looking for a fight.

Again.

I smirk, leaning against the doorjamb.

"River," I say coolly. "To what do I owe"—I trail my eyes up and down her body—"*this* pleasure?"

"Your awful, old-person music ruined my bath...*again!*"

I roll my eyes. "It's not even that loud."

"We've been over this time and time again, Dean. Your loud and my loud are two different things, especially when the walls are thin."

"If they were thin, I'd be able to hear *your* music through them."

"I don't play music."

"What do you mean you don't play music?"

"I mean, I don't play it. I'm not a music person. But that's not the point. The point is—"

"You're not a music person?" I curl my lip. "*Not a music person?* So you're a monster, then?"

"Don't you dare try to villainize me. *You're* the asshole in this situation."

"Because I'm listening to music. This sounds a whole lot like the plot of *Footloose* to me..."

"*Footloose* is about dancing."

"I'm not dancing for you, River."

"What? Ugh!" She groans, tossing her head back, her towel slipping down her breasts just a fraction of an inch. "I don't want you to dance for me. I'd rather cut off my big toe with a rusty spoon than watch you dance."

"That's not true. You've never seen me dance—I could have some sweet moves."

"I highly, *highly* doubt that. There's nothing sweet about you."

"Oh, River, I beg to differ."

"Beg all you want. It's the truth." She gives me a pointed look. "Just turn the fucking music down, Dean."

"You know what? No. I don't think I will."

"If you don't, I'm going to—"

"What? Report me to Lucy? Please. That woman loves me. She never does anything with the inane complaints."

"She should take them seriously. This building would be a lot better off without the likes of you."

"With you still here? Not likely."

"Come *on.* You're the nuisance, not me."

I raise a brow at her. "Says the girl who constantly *tattles* on her neighbors. Even my students know tattling isn't cool."

"I don't tattle, but now that you mention it, I feel awful for those poor, misguided gremlins who have to suffer through the school year with *you* as their teacher."

"I'll have you know I'm an excellent teacher."

She huffs. "Just like you're an excellent dancer."

"You know, I'm beginning to think the whole reason you came over here was to show off that tiny towel of yours. Does someone have a sexual agenda with me?"

"What? No! You are seriously insane! Utterly fucking deranged."

"I happen to think I'm perfectly sane."

Her eyes fall back to menacing slits as she takes a step toward me. I'd be terrified if she weren't eight inches shorter than me...and turning me on so much. "Turn. The. Music. Down."

I invade her space right back. "No."

"Turn it down, Dean."

"Make me."

"Fine."

She's fast; I'll give her that.

River pushes past me like it's no obstacle at all, sprinting into my apartment.

"Where is it?"

"Son of a..." I chase after her.

"Where's your ster—FIRE! Fire! Fire! Fire!"

"What?" I barely stop myself from crashing into her when the smell hits me. "Shit! Fire!"

I grab the spray hose connected to the sink and aim for the fire.

"No! Don't! Water—"

I spray.

And everything goes to hell in a handbasket.

Flames lick over the stove, across the towel that's disintegrating into nothing, and up the wall. It feels like it happens in less than two seconds.

"You idiot!" River pulls on me to get back. "Water and grease do not play well together!"

"Why didn't you tell me that before?"

"I tried! Why don't you know that?"

"Stop arguing and go call nine-one-one!"

She races from the apartment, and I head for the couch, jerking a blanket from the back, throwing it over the fire.

It seems to work...for a moment.

Then the flames burst through the material. We need to get out of here immediately.

"We need to go *now!*" River shrieks as she comes barreling back in, echoing my thoughts. She yanks on me, trying to pull me out of the apartment. "Come on! Move it!"

"Wait! I need to grab Leo."

"*Oh my gosh!* HURRY UP!"

I move like lightning, scooping Leo out of his terrarium and back into his on-the-go hut. "Sorry you're back in here, buddy. Just trying to save your life."

"Will you quit talking to your turtle and move it already? I *really* don't want to die in here with *you*."

"Why are you still here?" I fire back at her. "That concerned about my safety?"

"Because I'm a good person."

"Doubt that." I fasten the lid. "Done. Let's go." I hold my hand out to her, and she scoffs at it.

"Please. I am *not* holding your hand, Dean."

I ignore her and grab her hand anyway, pulling her from the apartment and away from the still growing fire.

"Wait!"

We stop, and River reaches for the fire alarm, yanking it down.

She grins up at me. "I've always wanted to do that."

She tightens her grip on me, and I can already hear the sirens outside as I try to ignore the way I like how her hand feels in mine.

Chapter 5

RIVER

"THE GOOD NEWS is whoever threw the blanket on the flames helped contain the fire and it didn't spread past the apartment."

I let out a heavy breath. Seeing as I'm his next-door neighbor and the most likely to sustain damage, I'm relieved by the firefighter's words.

"Ha!" Dean points to me like he's the smartest man alive, feeling extra proud of himself for helping contain the fire *he* started.

"But whoever threw water on the grease wasn't too bright and could have burned the entire building down."

I don't even bother trying to hide my smirk as Dean cowers into himself, full of embarrassment.

Good. Moron.

Who doesn't know that the one thing you definitely *do not* do is throw water on a grease fire?

And to think he's teaching our youths...

Though, if I am being one hundred percent fair...I didn't know this until I *also* threw water on a grease fire and almost burned my own house down.

Suppose Dean and I now have something in common.

Technically, two things: grease fires and pie.

But I'm not giving him the satisfaction of ever admitting my mistake out loud.

Dean looks to the firefighter. "What's the bad news?"

"You burned your apartment."

"Fully aware." His teeth gnash together, jaw tight with frustration. "I meant—"

"Is that a turtle?" the firefighter interrupts, pointing to Leo, who is sitting between us in his hut at the back of the ambulance. "Were there any other pets inside the apartment?"

"Just Leo here."

"You named your turtle Leo?" The man huffs. "How original."

"Thank you!" I toss my hands up. "That's what I said!"

"He's actually named after Tolstoy."

"Uh-huh. I'm sure that's what you were going for and you didn't just come up with that after you named your turtle after the Ninja Turtle and people made fun of you for it."

"I don't have to answer to you, especially when you're dressed like a baked potato." Dean's eyes drift down my body.

I don't get the same chills I got when he raked that gaze over my towel-clad body earlier. The hair on my arms doesn't stand on end, and my whole being doesn't tingle with something I haven't felt in a *really* long time.

No. Now, I'm mortified.

I look ridiculous.

Like the idiot I am, so wrapped up in my anger at Dean, I ran next door to yell at him in nothing but my towel.

By the time I'd realized it, it was too late to turn back. He was opening the door, and I am not one to back down from a challenge—no matter how ridiculously dressed I am.

Then the fire happened, and the last thing on my mind was putting on clothes. I just wanted out of the burning building because the last person I want to die next to is *him*.

Now I'm standing at the back of the ambulance wrapped in some spacesuit-like blanket looking like a fool while our neighbors glare at us for ruining their day.

I'm glad Caroline is at work and isn't around to witness this—though I'm sure Cooper, who is trying his damnedest to hold back a smirk, will relay the debacle in complete detail.

I give him a wave, and he tips his head to the side.

You okay? he mouths, like the gentleman he is.

I shoot him a thumbs-up and he grins, accepting my answer.

Like I can feel his eyes on me, I glance up at Dean, who's staring down at me with a look I can't quite decipher.

"What?"

Ignoring me, he turns back to the firefighter. "What's the damage?"

"Your apartment is burned." The firefighter laughs when Dean's face twists with frustration. "I'm just screwing with you, kid. Sometimes you have to find a way to laugh on a tough job like this."

He doesn't respond, just stares at the first responder with unamused eyes.

The guy clears his throat. "Well, like I said, the fire was semi-contained, so much of the damage is to the kitchen. However, because of the open concept of the apartment, my men are reporting that part of the living room was damaged as well."

"Leo's terrarium?"

"Your wannabe Ninja Turtle's house is intact."

Dean lets out a relieved breath, one I'm certain he's been holding since we ran from the building. I can't imagine Leo's setup is cheap, and since my mother was a teacher, I am more than aware of how little he makes.

"I'm happy to hear that. I'm glad Leo's okay." Lucy makes everyone jump by appearing out of thin air like she frequently does.

"Aw, crap. Lucy, I am *so* sorry. I didn't...I wasn't thinking. River came barging over to my apartment under the guise of *another* noise complaint when I'm certain she was just lonely and needed company but was too afraid to ask. I—"

"You ass!" I yell at him, trying hard not to smack him upside his head.

He just smirks down at me, and I shrink into myself.

I'm sure me showing up in a towel didn't help at all, but that is *so* not what I was doing there.

Dean ruined yet another day of mine—first by stealing my pie, then by getting me all riled up and stressed when I'm already stressed. Next he had to go and ruin my bath. The *one* thing I had going for me today, he screws up.

This whole thing is his fault, and I refuse to take any of the blame for it.

Nope. Not going to happen.

Ever.

Lucy pats Dean's shoulder. "Don't sweat it, dear. I'm just glad everyone is okay, the damage was contained, and the apartment below you was empty. We'll let insurance take care of everything." The corners of her lips tip down. "I am sorry about you having to find new living arrangements."

"Is the apartment not habitable at all?"

"It is. However, as building manager, *I* can't have you staying there, for insurance purposes. I'm sure you understand."

Dean's face falls, all the color vanishing in a flash.

His shoulders slump as the reality of everything starts to set in.

"I'll hold the apartment for you once things get back in tiptop shape," Lucy tells him.

"Oh, hell. Fucking hell. Where am I going to live? There's no way I'd ever go back to my parents', and my best friend's place is way too small for the two of us and Leo." His eyes widen with fear. "Leo! Ah, crap, crap, crap. I could go to a hotel but...oh, hell. Shit. I am completely screwed. I—"

"Dean," Lucy says in that soothing voice of hers as he gulps in air. "We'll figure it out. Just take a breath. Relax."

"Relax? I can't relax, Lucy! I just almost burned down your entire building!"

"Oh, dear..." She steers him a few feet away, talking softly, trying to get him to cool off.

The firefighter whistles. "I've been in this business long enough to know insurance can move slow as all heck. It could be a rough couple of months for him."

Months? Dean could be out of a place to live for that long? And Leo too?

Shit. That makes me feel bad for Leo.

And I guess Dean too.

But only by default.

"Damn. Tough break for him." The gentleman shakes his head, then turns to me, hitching his thumb toward his crew. "I'll send one of my men over to finish up taking your statements. You just let me know if you need anything else."

"Thanks," I murmur, shooting him a quick smile, then diverting my gaze back to the scene in front of me.

It's hard to take my eyes off Dean.

He towers over Lucy, his head in his hands as she speaks to him in hushed tones.

He's more upset than I've ever seen him before—and that includes the time his football team lost the big game...or whatever it was he cried about for a week.

I'm sure everything coming up in the next few months is running through his head on a loop, including summer school, which he's scheduled to start teaching in a couple weeks.

A nagging feeling starts at the base of my spine and slides up my neck.

Crap.

Maybe I *do* feel bad for him, and not just because he's Leo's handler.

I like little Leo, not that I'd ever admit it, and I don't want Dean to have to give him up just so he can have a place to stay. That's not fair to either of them.

I do have a spare room...

No! That's ludicrous.

I can*not* have Dean staying with me. There is absolutely zero good that can come of it. We'll kill each other.

There's no way we'd survive it.

But Leo...

"He can stay with me!"

They swivel their heads my way, and I slap my hand over my mouth as my words register in my own ears.

What the fuck did I just say?

Dean lifts that one brow he always lifts, cocking his head to the side. I hate that brow. "What was that?"

"You can stay with me."

No! Stop talking, River!

"What?"

I groan, pulling my spacesuit tighter around me, suddenly feeling more exposed than when all I had covering my body was the world's tiniest towel.

"Do not make me say it again, you ass."

"No, I don't think I heard you. I—"

"Unless your head's filled with as much smoke as your apartment is"—Lucy sasses, making him cringe—"you heard her perfectly fine, dear." She moves toward me, clapping her hands together with a smile on her lips that I decidedly do not like. "*That* is a wonderful idea, River."

"You cannot be serious." Dean comes up beside her. "There's no way you're serious."

"I am."

Holy shit.

I *am* serious.

I'm willing to let Dean stay with me.

It's just a month or two, right? I'm sure I can keep from murdering him for that long.

"Are you Punking me? Ashton? Ashton Kutcher? You can come out now!"

I purse my lips. "Yes, because I brought Ashton Kutcher here to screw with you and not to screw him myself. In your dreams, idiot."

"That would be in *your* dreams."

I huff, and Lucy laughs.

"Oh, yes." She smashes her lips together, trying to hold in a grin. "This is going to work out perfectly."

"I want a contract." I point at her. "Like a good one. A legit one. Something that's going to keep that menace from freeloading off me for the rest of his days."

"There are so many things wrong with that statement. The first one is that you actually think *I'm* the menace."

"You're the one who plays music way too loud! That's exactly what got you into this mess!"

"No, what got me into this mess was you waltzing over to my apartment looking sexy in nothing but a freaking towel."

"Did you just call me *sexy*?"

"You were wearing a towel, River. A. Towel! I'm a man— I'd think Lucy was sexy in a towel!" Dean winces. "I mean, no offense, Lucy. It's just...you're as old as my grandmother..."

"None taken." She waves her hand. "But just so you know, I look damn sexy in a towel."

She waggles her brows, and Dean's eyes grow to twice their usual size.

"I-I..." He flounders, trying to find the right words to say. "I...umm..."

Lucy ignores Dean being...well, Dean.

"You can have your contract, River. I will start working on it tonight and get everything squared away tomorrow morning. What needs to happen now is everyone getting back to their apartments and getting on with their day. You two need to rest. You've had a long day, and a good night's rest is certainly in order." She smiles slyly. "It may be a few people's last chance at that."

I groan.

"Why do I absolutely hate the way that sounds?"

"Because, dear, I'm likely right. Now, let me get everything wrapped up with those nice firefighters and we'll all be back inside before we know it. Be right back."

Lucy scurries away, leaving me and Dean alone.

Which I guess I should get used to because *apparently* he's going to be living with me now.

Why did I say he could stay with me? Why couldn't I just keep my big mouth shut? Damn Leo for making me feel bad.

I glare at the turtle, who looks not so happy about being back in his hut.

"Don't give him evil eyes. He didn't do anything to you."

"Because he's a turtle, not a person."

"He has plenty of personality, which is more than I can say for you." He sneers at me.

"I am *full* of personality—and sparkling personality at that. I'm a fucking ray of sunshine."

"Oh, I highly doubt that."

"Is that how you're choosing to talk to me? The person who is kind enough to allow you to live in her apartment when you have a history of arson?"

Dean works his jaw back and forth. He wants to say something snarky, but he bites his tongue.

Smart man.

The first responders release everyone else back to their apartments. Most of our neighbors give us sad smiles as they shuffle back inside, but a few of them send daggers our way.

"It was all him." I point at Dean. "Direct your fury at this guy."

Dean smacks my finger away. "Stop that. We've been over this: you distracted me with—"

"My towel—yeah, I've heard. You know, you keep bringing that up. It's almost as if you have a little crush on me or something."

He scoffs. "I already told you, I'd find anyone attractive in a towel."

"Whatever you need to tell yourself to help you sleep in the room across from me at night. Speaking of that…" I push myself up from the ambulance, facing him. "This whole you-moving-in thing is completely temporary."

"That was my understanding too."

"It's just until your place gets fixed or you find other accommodations."

He narrows his eyes. "Yeah, I got that."

"And there will be rules."

He exhales. "I figured as much."

"Good. I just want to make myself clear."

"You're clear."

I turn on my heel and start to head back into the building —then something hits me.

Dean said I was sexy.

A line needs to be drawn ASAP.

I turn back to him, and he looks at me with curious eyes.

"Yes, River?" Up goes the brow.

"You can't try to sleep with me."

He drops his jaw, stunned by what I've said.

Then, he bursts into laughter.

And not just any sort of laughter.

No. It's the loud kind, the type that draws *every* eye in a hundred-foot radius.

That's exactly what's happening—*everyone* is looking over at us as he doubles over.

"Seriously?" I scowl, waiting for him to get himself together.

When he finally comes up for air, he's swiping at his eyes like he's brushing back tears.

"Oh, man. Thank you for that. I needed a good laugh. It's been a long day." Dean pushes up from the ambulance, grabbing Leo's hut. He stalks toward me with confidence. "Don't worry, River, I'm not going to have an issue resisting you."

"Not even in"—I drop the spacesuit—"this?"

Dean's eyes darken the moment the blanket hits the ground, his jaw clenching tightly as his nostrils flare.

He tries, I'll give him that.

But he can't fight it.

Slowly, his eyes drift down my body, and just like earlier, I can feel his gaze stroking all over me.

Except this time, it's *more.*

It's almost like I'm wearing nothing.

Like he can see *all* of me.

Even the parts I hide.

I regret tossing the blanket aside for only a moment.

Then power washes through me, and for once during the little game of back-and-forth we've been playing over the last year, I'm the one in control.

Dean is always the one to get the last word in. He's always the one to walk away, leaving me feeling flustered and annoyed.

Not today.

No, I won't give him the satisfaction

I lift my chin, not backing down. "Looks like that might not be the case after all, Dean."

I spin on my heel, leaving him standing there staring after me.

And I know he is.

Because his stare is just as hot as the fire he set.

Chapter 6

I'VE BEEN LIVING with River for all of five minutes and I already want to move out.

Not just because she's the reincarnation of Lucifer, of which I'm ninety-nine percent certain, especially after that stunt she pulled outside.

Or because I'm her sworn enemy for some reason unknown to me.

It's none of those things.

It's the damn cat.

The one who's been sitting perched on the couch, hissing at me for the last few minutes. The same one who's snuck out of River's apartment no less than ten times over the past year and found his way inside of mine, trying to get to Leo.

When I attempt to pick him up and take him home, he goes on the defense like *I'm* the one invading *his* space.

"Morris, be nice." River sets one of my suitcases near the couch, reaching over and scratching between his ears. "Once he gets to know you, he'll mellow out." She pauses, shooting a glance my way. "Well, maybe not. It is *you*, after all."

"Is that any way to treat a guest?" I roll my other suitcase next to the first.

The firefighter was right about the fire damage: it was mostly contained to the kitchen, only a small spot in the living area burned.

The biggest killer was the smoke damage. It's evident throughout the entire apartment. I'm not a big fan of keeping doors closed—makes me feel all boxed in—so it spread fast and far.

I'm certain I'm going to have to wash all the clothes I tossed into suitcases at least twice just to get the stench out.

A fire. A damn grease fire at that.

I could have burned the entire building down today.

I could have hurt myself. Or Leo.

River.

Fuck, I am such a moron.

I glance around my new living space. Aside from a few color changes like different flooring and cabinetry, it's the exact unit I have—had—just flipped.

Should be a relatively easy adjustment. That's good, because I could use something easy considering I just set my apartment on fire and all.

Shit. I can't believe River of all people took me in.

My sister's place was a bust, considering she's still living back in Assholetown.

Nolan's place is way too small, and sketchy. The dude should move to a better neighborhood.

And there's no way in hell I'll be going to my parents with this. My dad would eat this mishap up like it's bacon, and my old man fucking loves bacon.

A hotel would have been my only other option, and it would have been an expensive one. When River offered up her place, I almost said no. I'd pony up that money just to spite her kindness. But then the thought of picking up my life and moving into a complete unknown for an indefinite number of weeks when I have so much on my plate coming up…

And, well, here I am.

Fucking hell. I scrub a hand through my hair, pulling at the ends a little too hard. But, shit, I mean, how dumb am I to let myself get into this mess? With my luck, this is going to take months to fix. It's going to completely throw off Leo's schedule, *my* schedule. It's—

"Hey." River's voice interrupts my panic. "Everything will be fine. Lucy was right—nobody was hurt, and that's the most important thing. Apartments and things are replaceable. People and pets aren't. Just focus on that and everything else will fall into place."

Her words are soft. Calming even, like she can read the anxiety flowing through my mind. It's the sweetest her tone has ever been toward me.

"Uh, thanks." I lift a hand, squeezing the back of my neck. It's strange being on the receiving end of niceness from River.

Yet…it's comforting.

"You're welcome." She clears her throat, then points toward the console resting against the wall. "You can put Leo over here if that works for you. You'll be staying in my office, and there's no spot for a tank in there. I'll go in and rearrange it tomorrow so there's room for more than just an air mattress. You'll have to sleep on the couch for tonight."

"I don't mind the couch. Some nights I pass out on mine anyway. I'm just thankful to have a place to stay."

And it's true.

Even if it is with River.

She nods and begins pulling knickknacks off the console, moving them to the bookshelf taking up the other wall. "I don't have much food here and I was planning on pie for dinner, so we'll need to grocery shop too."

"I can pay for those. It can be part of my rent for staying here. Which, again, I appreciate."

Another short nod. "And I'll need to stop by the hardware store sometime to get you a key. Maya has my only spare."

She moves on quickly again, like she doesn't want me to acknowledge her niceness at all.

I just don't get why.

"What's your angle?"

She halts her movements, peeking up at me through the messy red hair that's barely staying in the clip she has it thrown up in. "Excuse me?"

"I said, what's your angle? Why are you letting me stay here and then acting all whatever about it when I keep trying to thank you?"

Her brows go up a fraction. "Is that what you're doing?"

"Yes."

"It doesn't seem that way."

"Doesn't it?"

Another fraction.

I clench my jaw. "Thank you, River. Thank you for allowing me to stay here. I'm not sure how I'll ever repay you."

One hand on her hip, she taps her finger to her chin. "Gee, I wonder how you could repay me. Other than rent—because I fully expect that." She snaps her fingers. "I got it! How about you stop stealing my pie."

I narrow my eyes. "No."

"Looks like someone's going to be homeless, then."

"Do you *really* think I'm buying that the whole reason you're allowing me to stay here is so I stop 'stealing' your pie?"

"The fact that you just put stealing in air quotes…" She shakes her head, her anger palpable. "Stop questioning my motives."

"So you're admitting you have motives?"

"What? No."

"Then what is this?"

She growls, tossing her head back in frustration. "Why are you overanalyzing it? Can't you just be grateful?"

"That's what I was *trying* to do, and you were being dismissive."

"Because you're acting weird." She shoves past me and to the bookshelf, setting yet another figurine on it.

Geez, how many of these things does she have?

"Weird how?"

"I don't know…nice."

"I'm always nice to you. I buy you pie."

She slams the statue down, pushing past me again, grabbing two more and walking them back to the shelf. "You buy me pie because you feel guilty for taking mine. That's not being nice—that's covering your own ass."

She has me there…

"Okay, so there might be some truth to that. But, still. I consider you a friend, River." She snorts. "Maybe not a friend, but at least an acquaintance."

After placing the last two collectibles on the shelf where she wants them, she turns to me.

Her plump mouth is drawn into a thin line. Even though she looks serious, I can't help but let my eyes wander.

I've checked River out plenty in the past.

I'd be a fool not to acknowledge how attractive she is.

But after seeing her in that towel, it's like I can't take my eyes away from her.

She's ditched her scrap of near nothing and exchanged it for a pair of navy leggings and an oversized shirt. Her hair is the same mess it was, and she's still not wearing a stitch of makeup. She spent her afternoon trying to put out a literal fire I set and yet…she looks incredible.

She takes two steps toward me, and I drag my eyes from her body to her hazel stare.

"You're a pain in my ass. Loud and obnoxious. The world's worst neighbor." I open my mouth, but she points at me. "You *just* tried to burn the apartment building down, so don't even try to refute that." I nod. "We've established that I hate you. We are *not* friends. We're neighbors, and right now, we're roommates. That's *it*. Nothing else. So don't go getting any notions in your head that I'm going to fall for your charms and we'll end up buds anytime soon. You do your thing, I'll do mine."

I want to argue.

Mostly for the sake of arguing.

But she's right. The easiest way for us to navigate this without butting heads every five minutes is to just stick to our respective corners.

"Got it?"

I give her a nod. "Understood."

"Good." She turns on her heel and makes her way to the front door. Slides her shoes on. "Let's hit the store."

"I thought you said we're supposed to do our own thing."

She grits her teeth, not liking my smartass comment. "All this excitement for the day has made me hungry." She pulls open the door. "And you ruined my pie, so you owe me dinner. Let's go."

My stomach growls at the mention of food, and I realize I am *starving* because I never did get to eat that damn sandwich.

I grab Leo's hut. "At least let me pick the place."

She tosses me a look. "It's cute that you think that's how this works."

"Anyone ever tell you you're a little short to be this sassy?"

"Just shut up and feed me before I get hangry."

"This is you *normally*? Man, it's going to be a blast living with you, then."

She grumbles something I can't quite make out, but whatever it is, it doesn't sound as grumpy as I expect.

I get the feeling River isn't going to hate having me as a roommate as much as she thinks she will.

"DO you mind if we stop in at the pet store for a minute? I need to grab a few things for Leo's terrarium."

One of the perks of the apartment building we live in is the location. It's a primo spot right in the heart of the city. Nearly everything important is within walking distance, and if it's not, you can bike. If you're feeling frisky, you can drive.

After (naturally) stopping by The Gravy Train for dinner —it's just down the block—we opted to walk to the store since we weren't doing hefty grocery shopping...or so I thought.

I'm carrying three bags—one on each shoulder and one in my hand—and River has one.

She bought no less than three pints of ice cream, not to mention at least four different kinds of cheese crackers.

I'm beginning to think she doesn't spend much time at home and doesn't eat there often either, which would make sense because the woman is always working. It's a miracle she ever found the time to complain about me when she was hardly home.

"Did you just ask if I was cool with going into the pet store? Where I get to play with the animals?"

"I'll take that as a yes."

"*Big* yes. Just don't tell Morris I got excited about it."

"Won't he smell it on you?"

"Yes, but I'll just tell him it's your fault."

"And he'll...believe that?"

"Yeah." She shrugs. "He's as gullible as Sam is."

I chuckle...and only kind of worry for her sanity. "Sam's a good kid."

"He's the best kid. Like ever."

"You're biased."

"I'm allowed to be biased. He's been part of my life for nearly half of it." She cocks her head. "What? Your eyes just widened."

"It's nothing. I just never considered how old Sam is in relation to how old Maya is. I'm assuming we're around the same age, so..."

"You're just now putting together that Maya had a teenage pregnancy." She nods. "She gets that look a lot."

"I didn't mean anything by it. Truly."

"Oddly enough, I believe that," she mutters, hefting the reusable bag—the one she made me buy because it was *cute* and I *owed her*—higher.

"Do you need help with your one bag?"

She ignores me. "I'm twenty-eight. Is that how old you are?"

"Yep. As of last month."

"What? I didn't know it was your birthday last month!"

"How would you? We're not friends, not acquaintances. Just neighbors, remember?"

Her brows slide together, not liking how I throw her words back in her face. "Whatever. It's nothing personal. I just like birthdays."

"I'll file that info away in my *Things I Now Know About My Neighbor Who Hates Me* folder for future non-interactions."

I get a scowl for that one.

I stop in front of the pet store doors and turn to River. "Look, there are a lot of cute fluffy things in here."

"Like...gerbils? And bunnies? And guinea pigs?" She gasps. "Oh my gosh, where do guinea pigs even live in the wild? I've literally never thought of that until this very moment. Where do gerbils live? What even *is* a gerbil?"

She's talking a mile a minute and I already regret asking her if we can stop, but I need things for Leo's terrarium. I hope River doesn't mind me taking over her bathroom tonight to scrub out his tank and get it cleaned so I can start replacing things.

"We have frozen stuff," I remind her. "Like that pint of ice cream you stole right out of my hands."

She lifts a shoulder. "Should have put it in your bag faster."

She's lucky it was only my third-favorite flavor; otherwise I'd have made a scene.

"But I understand. I won't take too much time playing with all the adorable little creatures."

"Why do I not believe you at all?"

"Because I'm likely lying." She breezes past me, pulling the door open. She glances back over her shoulder, loose tendrils of her red hair blowing in the breeze. "Come on. I don't want my ice cream to melt."

What the hell have I gotten myself into?

Chapter 7

RIVER

A CRIME SCENE IS IMMINENT.

Dean has been living in my apartment for all of two days, and I am close to kicking his sorry ass to the curb. Or just skipping right to murdering him.

I slam the refrigerator closed and turn to him, glaring.

He sets his fork down beside his nearly empty breakfast plate and rubs his tired eyes. "What now?"

"You know what."

He rakes his fingers through his inky hair. "Look, I slept like ass last night, so if you could just get on with whatever accusation it is you have this time, I'd appreciate it."

"And I'd appreciate if you stopped using all of my creamer."

It's not the first thing of mine he's used either.

When I woke up yesterday, he was digging into my eggs. Sure, they're only eggs, but we'd *just* gone to the grocery store the night before and argued over how the grocery system would work.

It took ten minutes of practically screaming at one another in the chip aisle, but we managed to agree that he would buy his own groceries—and only his own—and we'd divide the fridge evenly.

Apparently, his version of evenly and mine were two different things.

Even though the shop is closed on Mondays, I fled to the boutique so I could avoid him.

Turns out, him eating my eggs was only the first of many offenses to come.

Like leaving his sweaty, smelly socks sitting inside his shoes after the gym. I had to light *two* candles just to get the stink out of the living room.

Then there's his constant bickering with Morris, who Dean *clearly* hates. (It's fine. The feeling is mutual.)

And the biggest complaint of all: I can't just walk in the door and pop my bra off.

My back is starting to hurt, and these bad boys need to be free. He's screwing with my ability to come home and relax at night.

Well, to be fair, he's always done that.

But this is worse.

"I didn't use your creamer, River."

I nod toward his mug, which contains coffee that is far from straight black. "Then what's in your cup?"

"Coffee."

"Coffee *and*…"

"Sunshine.

"Dean."

"It's milk."

I sniff. "You expect me to believe that when my creamer is obviously empty?"

"I'm not the only person in this apartment. Did you stop to think *you* might have used the last of your creamer?"

"No. I'd know."

"If that were the case, you'd remember when we were at the grocery store two days ago and you stood in front of the creamer for five minutes picking one out and then putting it back because you *still had plenty at home*."

He says it so confidently I almost believe him.

"You almost had me, but I distinctly remember putting it in my bag."

"Then you took it out when we went down the ice cream aisle because if you ran out of creamer, you'd just stop by The Gravy Train." He sighs again. "Trust me, I did not steal your shit."

"I don't believe you."

He pushes up from the chair and grabs his plate, taking it to the sink. "That's too damn bad, because it's the truth."

I cross my arms, leaning against the counter, watching him.

He rolls the sleeves of his dress shirt in a way that makes his forearms pop, especially when he reaches for the sponge. He lightly scrubs his plate, then pops it into the dishwasher before moving on to the other dishes in the sink.

"You don't need to do that. That's my mess—I can clean it up."

He ignores me and continues to pre-wash all the dishes like the dishwasher wasn't invented to do that exact job.

Whatever. If he wants to double-wash everything, he can waste his time.

His bottom lip is tucked between his teeth as he concentrates on what he's doing.

The smell of something that most definitely is *not* dish soap washes over me.

It's Dean.

Cinnamon and cedarwood.

The spice comes from that damn gum he's always chewing, and the woodsy scent must be from his cologne.

I find myself wanting to lean into him, to get better acquainted with the fragrance, because I've never smelled a combination so enticing before.

He makes a noise, and I realize I'm just standing here watching and sniffing him like a creep.

What the hell am I doing? Why am I still standing here? Just walk away, River...

Except for some reason, I don't.

"So, any plans for the day?" I ask.

"I'm heading to school today to start getting my classroom ready for classes next week. It was on my agenda before the fire."

"You teach English, right?"

"Yep."

"Sam said it was his favorite class last year. Surprising, because that kid hates reading."

A smile curves over Dean's lips. "I like hearing that. Sam's a good student. He always asked such...interesting questions about the reading assignments. Came at them from an unexpected angle a lot of times. Surprised me, something that's harder to do the longer I teach."

"Have you been teaching long?"

"About four years now. I worked at my father's company straight out of high school for a while, but it wasn't what I wanted to do. I quit, enrolled in school, and have been teaching since."

"Do you like it?"

"I love it. Don't get me wrong, it has its bad days, but every job does." He shrugs. "Can't imagine myself doing much else."

I can understand that. It's how I feel about Making Waves.

"Why'd you sleep like shit last night?"

Another sigh as he peeks over at me. "Why are you asking so many questions?"

"Because I'm my most curious in the mornings." I give him a sarcastic smile.

He's right; I *am* asking a lot of questions, and I'm not sure why. I'm feeling unusually chatty—but maybe I'm always this chatty and I just don't know it because there's never anyone else here.

I should stop while I'm ahead. I don't want to get comfortable having someone here to talk to. More than that, I don't want Dean getting too comfortable here.

He finally answers me. "I never truly fell into a deep sleep."

"I didn't keep you up, did I?"

Thick brows go up, a teasing smirk on his lips. "Do you mean the first, second, or third time you came into the office?"

I flew in at eleven PM, just fifteen minutes after Dean had retired for the night, and flipped the light right on.

I didn't even think about him being in there. It was completely out of habit.

He jumped off his air mattress wearing only a pair of gray boxer briefs that left *nothing* to the imagination.

I averted my eyes as quickly as I could, but not before getting a look at what he had to offer.

There was a moment when I questioned why I hated him again.

Then, he spoke.

"Fucking hell. I thought you were a gremlin. Then I got a good look at you."

"And?"

"Gremlins are cuter."

I flipped him off, grabbed the notebook I was after, and left without turning the light off.

I could hear him cursing as I scurried back to my room.

The other times I went in there weren't even out of spite. I genuinely needed things. It was just a bonus that it interrupted his sleep.

But seeing him this morning... Guilt sits heavy in my stomach, especially since I can relate to how unrested he's feeling.

I've suffered from insomnia for several years now. If I'm being honest, I can pinpoint it back to when I started my business. It's the daily stress of knowing this could all crumble at any second, knowing there are two other employees banking on my business working.

These thoughts *literally* keep me up at night.

Silly with the shop doing as well as it is, but also valid because, hey, it's doing well. In my experience, that means it's all going to come crashing down at any moment.

It was at Maya's insistence that I finally saw my doctor about it last year. Though I'm not generally one for taking medication, I knew if I wanted to be successful, I needed to sleep more than three *interrupted* hours a night.

I hate taking it, hate being dependent on it—or on anything, for that matter. So, I do everything else I can to avoid it. Yoga, meditation, cutting back on screen time, anything other than giving up my work that helps reduce stress.

For the most part, it works. I'm not taking my medication nearly as often now.

Dean is still staring at me expectantly, so I just shrug. "I'm not used to having someone in there, and I needed to check on a few things."

He lifts that damn brow again, not buying it, even though it's true.

I did struggle last night knowing he was in the other room, but only because I'm honestly not used to having someone else in my apartment.

It has nothing to do with the fact that the someone is Dean.

He's nobody to me. Just my neighbor from hell.

"I'll bring my work laptop home tonight so I don't bug you again."

"Thank you." He starts scrubbing another dish. "Do you always work so late at night?"

I shrug. "Sometimes. Usually when I can't sleep, or if a new idea hits me."

"Is your boutique that busy?"

His words put me on edge.

I don't like them. They're condescending. Like my livelihood doesn't matter as much as his precious sleep.

Like my shop is a joke to him.

I push off the counter, bustling out of the kitchen and

down the hallway to my bedroom to finish getting ready for work.

Maybe if I distract myself, I won't kill him.

Not killing him would probably be best.

I think.

Sliding onto the stool at my vanity, I begin finagling my hair into place. I pull it up into a neat bun, but I don't like the look. Too severe.

I try a messy one, and it's too…well, messy.

I yank the hairband out, hating everything I try.

My outfit catches my eye in the mirror, and I hate that too.

No. Stop it. You're just letting Dean get to you. You love this outfit. It's your favorite. It's him. *That's all.*

I close my eyes and take a deep, calming breath.

If Dean's going to be living here, I need to add more yoga to my routine to help keep me from exploding.

I can't keep letting him get to me. He isn't worth the frustration.

He doesn't matter.

"River."

I peel my eyes open, surprised to find Dean standing in my doorway. He's leaning against the jamb, arms crossed. That damn dress shirt is pulled taut against his chest.

Why does he look so good in it?

"I have a distinct feeling you took my words the wrong way."

"Did I?"

He nods. "Yes. I didn't mean anything by it. I just meant…well, I'm not entirely sure. I guess I just didn't realize your little boutique was so…time-consuming."

I huff, pushing to my feet.

If I don't leave now, I am seriously going to maim him.

He puts his arm up, blocking me from passing by.

"Let me through."

"I didn't mean anything by that either."

I glare up at him. "Then what *do* you mean, Dean?"

"I don't know. I'm not certain what I'm trying to say, and frankly, I'm worried that no matter what I say, it's going to offend you."

"You're probably right."

"Can I get that in writing?"

"Dean."

"Fine. Let me start over, then?" He clears his throat. "It's sad you stay up so late working on your business, but I don't mean that in a bad way. I mean it like...I wish you were able to delegate more so you didn't have to sacrifice sleep...or interrupt mine."

I knew there would be selfish reasons for his words. I open my mouth, but he beats me to the punch.

"But I also understand not wanting to hand over your baby to someone else. On the flip side of that, it's a huge accomplishment that your shop is doing so well. You should be proud. I am."

It's on the tip of my tongue to tell him to bite me and force my way past. I don't need his validation.

It's likely sad that my first instinct is to not believe him.

It's also likely childish of me.

But, hey, Dean brings out that side of me.

I nod a thanks, because deep down I think there's some sincerity to his words beyond him wanting uninterrupted sleep, and then I try to leave.

He doesn't let me.

I grit my teeth. "What?"

"Are we good?"

I roll my shoulders back and look up at him.

There's no way he misses the hitch in my breath.

His vibrant Kelly green eyes nearly knock me on my ass.

He looks genuinely worried that he's offended me.

He's never looked at me like this before, and that's saying something because he's offended me multiple times over the months he's been my neighbor.

This time feels different.

Like he cares.

About me.

For me.

My breaths begin to come in sharper, and if he notices, he doesn't give any indication.

"River, are we good?"

My eyes drift to his mouth…to his perfectly sculpted lips…

I bet they feel the way they look. *Soft.*

I wonder if he kisses the way he carries himself. *With confidence.*

I want to be kissed with confidence again.

All it would take is for me to push up onto my toes and I could test my theories…

No! Stop letting him affect you. He's still Dean.

"Are you just kissing ass because I'm providing you with housing?"

"Are you going to continually throw that in my face?"

"Yes."

He sighs, and I relent.

He's right. I do keep bringing it up, but I don't want him

to forget he's a guest here and, at any moment, I can take this away from him.

I'm the one on top this time.

I guess I could back off a bit… "No."

"Good." He nods once. "No, I'm not just saying it to kiss ass. I meant it."

"Well, thank you. I guess."

His lips tip up at the corners. "You're welcome. I guess."

I roll my eyes. "Can I go now? I need to get to work."

Slowly, he drops his arm, finally allowing me to pass.

I do, giving him a wide berth.

I need space. Apparently being close to him makes me realize ridiculous things like how good he smells. Or worse… how I wouldn't push him away if he tried to kiss me.

"Hey, River?"

I peer over my shoulder.

"I like your hair down."

I don't respond.

Instead, I continue through the apartment, scooping my long waves into a ponytail and twisting my hair tie around them.

Dean chuckles as I make my way out the door.

Chapter 8

DEAN

"CHEERS! Here's to International Childfree Day!"

"Is that a thing?"

"It is, though it's not technically for another month." Nolan, my best friend, tips his beer back.

"Why are we celebrating it today, then?"

"Because kid-free is the way to be, and I needed an excuse to indulge in some beer with my best friend."

"I'll drink to that." I clink my bottle to his.

"I've drunk to less."

I laugh. "True."

He wipes at his mouth with the back of his hand. "All right, so, let me get this straight: you're living with your neighbor."

"Yes."

"Who is hot as hell."

"She's…okay."

"Bullshit. I've seen her—she's hot."

"Ah, you've seen her, but have you *talked* to her for a long period? It definitely docks hotness points."

"Hot is hot." He rolls his eyes. "But what you're really trying to sit here and tell me is that living with your sexy neighbor is going to be the death of you because she *annoys you*?"

"Yes."

He shakes his head. "If anything, it's going to kill your sex life." He laughs to himself. "Just kidding…it's already dead."

"Fuck you very much, Nolan." I flip him the bird and lift my beer bottle to my lips, taking a swig.

I hate that he's not wrong.

My sex life *is* a joke. I don't remember the last time I went on a date that ended with me between two warm thighs instead of at home with my cock in my right hand.

It's been a long time. Too fucking long if you ask me.

The last girl I went out with spent the entire evening staring at her phone, and then she had the audacity to be offended when I suggested I take her home instead of back to my place.

Could I have taken her to my apartment and likely enjoyed a round or two in the sheets? There's no doubt about that.

But, shit, I like at least a little bit of decent conversation beforehand.

I'm not rushing to fall in love or anything, and I'm not saying I'm some heroic dude who hasn't ever taken a girl home just for sex; I'm just bored with the dating scene. There hasn't been a single girl I've gone out with who I've given a second thought to since…shit, I don't even know how long.

Nolan laughs. "Now, now, Mr. Evans, that's not very teacherly of you."

"Please." I set my bottle back in front of me, wrapping my fingers around it, picking at the blue and red label. "Everyone has these buttoned-up versions of teachers in their heads, but we're just as fucked up as the rest of 'em. We're simply better at hiding it."

"That's right. Don't want to startle the kiddos. Little twerps."

I chuckle. "One of these days, man, you're going to get knocked on your ass and end up with about ten of the little shits running around."

He scoffs. "Please. I know better than to get roped into that. That's eighteen years of responsibility." He curls his lips, disgusted by the idea. "No thanks."

"Right, Mr. Commitment-phobe. I forgot."

"At least I know what I do and don't want."

Ouch. "I don't think that's anything to brag about when you're always running after the honeymoon phase is over."

"That's what I call self-preservation."

"It's called being a wimp."

He doesn't acknowledge that, just tilts his beer back and finishes it off.

Because he knows I'm right.

I've known Nolan since I was five. We met at the bus stop for the same shitty school and bonded over neither of us having one of those sweet Power Ranger lunchboxes that were all the rage. All we had were brown paper sacks that were hardly bursting at the seams with nutritious treats.

Each day we'd meet up, and I'd swap my turkey and cheese for his peanut butter and jelly. He hated peanut butter, but it was all his dad could afford.

It never mattered to Nolan that my family won the lottery and we got out of that shithole.

He was still Nolan, and I was still Dean. That was that.

We've been close since we met. It's fair to say I know Nolan well, better than anyone.

It's how I know he's a runner and doesn't do commitment, which has everything to do with his mom bailing on his family when he was five. He's been a ball of bitterness and discontent ever since. In any relationship he's ever had, he's always left before he can be left.

I'm serious about him meeting some girl who'll knock him on his ass. It's going to happen, and I can't wait to be there to witness it.

"So, what's this chick doing now? Besides being an absolute angel by letting your dumb ass live there after you nearly burned your apartment building down."

I clench my jaw at the reminder, still pissed at myself—hence me sitting at the bar for happy hour, something I rarely do.

Like he could read my mind and knew I needed to blow off some steam, Nolan called me up and asked if I wanted to grab a beer. I jumped on the opportunity fast.

"She's accused me of stealing or using her things every day I've lived there."

"You've only been there for five days."

"I know." I laugh, but there's no humor to it because I don't find any of this funny. It's exhausting. "The first day, she was mad because I ate her eggs or some shit. The second, she was pissed because I apparently used all her creamer."

"Did you?"

"Yes." He chuckles. "The third *and* fourth day she was in a huff because I told her she shouldn't keep letting her dishes pile up in the sink. She hasn't spoken to me since."

"If you hate her that much, it sounds like the ideal situation, then."

"Oh, it'd be great, exactly what I want—except she still hasn't given me a key to the apartment."

Despite my asking her every day, she still hasn't given me a key. This means if I want to leave the apartment, I have to wait for her to get home so I can get back in. It's why I was on board for beers with Nolan. I had to be at the school today to help inventory the football equipment, and there was no way I'd be out late enough to warrant waiting around for River to come home.

I thought about stealing her keys and making a copy myself, but she keeps them in her room, and it felt wrong sneaking in there for them.

I do respect *some* of her boundaries.

"How do you still not have a key?"

I shrug. "No damn clue, man. I'm of the belief that it gives her some sort of high lording it over my head that she has the final say in when I come and go."

"Given everything you've told me about all your tiffs with her, that wouldn't surprise me. Still can't believe I haven't met her more than in passing yet."

"You should come over one night next week for a baseball game. You can meet her then."

"Two things." He holds a finger up. "One, baseball is boring as fuck, and you know I hate it." Another finger goes up. "Two, I'm in, but I do want to go on the record saying I don't think it's exactly good practice to invite strangers over to the place you're crashing at temporarily."

"One," I counter, "baseball *is* boring, but pizza and beer are not, and sports are an excuse for that. Two, I need a witness. I have a feeling either she or her cat is going to murder me."

"I'd never get in the way of a good murdering, especially when the asshole deserves it."

"So, you're in?"

"To watch your roommate-slash-enemy annihilate you?" He grins. "Fuck yeah." Nolan pushes his empty bottle away, shaking his head when the bartender motions toward it, asking if he wants another.

"Please. I'm not worried about River." I scoff, finishing off my beer.

"From what I've heard, you should be."

"I can deal with her."

"She seems feisty. Fun."

"She's…something."

Nolan tilts his head. "You said that in a funny way."

I draw my brows up. "What? I did not."

He eyes me, curious. Then, a slow smile curves over his lips. "Oh, fuck. Why didn't you tell me?"

"Tell you what?" I reach for the empty beer bottle, needing something to distract myself with, uncomfortable under his scrutiny. He's staring at me too hard and too long.

"That you have a thing for this chick."

I bark out a laugh, motioning to the bartender for another drink; I'm going to need one if I have to sit here and listen to Nolan's crap. "Please. I do not have a *thing* for her, whatever the fuck that's supposed to mean."

"It means she gets your dick *and* your other parts going." He leans in close and whispers, "You know, like *feelings* and shit."

"Whatever, man." I grab the beer the bartender silently

slides my way and take a hefty swig. I wipe my mouth with the back of my hand. "Is River hot? Yeah, sure. I'm not blind. She's the kind of girl I'd normally go for, but it's not a *thing*. The attraction is purely physical."

"Then you don't mind if I ask her out?"

"You don't even know her."

He grins, and I know he caught that my answer wasn't a flat-out no right off the bat. It *should* have been. We both know that.

"Hasn't stopped me before. I don't know a lot of the girls I go out with."

True. Nolan's not exactly the get-to-know-you type.

And whatever. I don't judge. It's not like I've never wined and dined for some pussy and then left before the awkward *Do you want to grab breakfast?*

The thought of him doing that to River...it makes my gut feel all weird. *Wrong.*

"If you don't have a thing for her, then she's fair game, right?"

"No."

The word tumbles from my lips on impulse, but that doesn't make it any less true.

If anything, it makes it all that much more honest.

I don't want to date River, but I don't want Nolan to date her either.

And I can't figure out why.

He laughs, then rises off his stool. "That's what I thought."

"Where are you going? What do you mean that's what you thought?"

"I'm heading out." He reaches into his back pocket,

93

pulling his wallet free and waving toward the bartender. "I've been up since the ass-crack of dawn. Not all of us get the summer off."

"Check?" The single word is the second time I've heard the bartender speak since I walked in here, and it's my favorite part about this bar. Nobody asks any questions or tries to therapize you. You can get a drink and be left alone.

Nolan nods, handing over his card, and the guy saunters off to take care of his tab.

"What did you mean that's what you thought?" I ask again when we're alone.

"Come on, man. Though I'm not sure why it's always the go-to when speaking about level of intelligence, it's not rocket science. You like her, and not just physically."

"No, I don't."

"You do," the bartender says, sliding Nolan's receipt across the counter before turning and leaving again.

"What the…" I glare at his retreating back, then shake my head. "He's wrong."

"He's not wrong." He signs the check and slides it back across the bar. "And I'm not either. You do like her. You just won't admit it to yourself for some reason. Maybe it's because you're staying there now and you don't want to rock the boat, which is smart, but you can't tell me you haven't thought about River before."

"I—"

"Not just when you're jacking your dick. I'm sure you do that plenty, you dirty dog."

Guilty as charged there.

It took every ounce of willpower I had not to wrap my hand around my cock that first night I was there. Every time I closed my eyes, all I could see was her in that tiny fucking towel, bent over so I could see everything she has to offer. The only thing that stopped me was knowing River was lying in bed across the hall and would hear me.

"I mean in a relationship kind of way."

He's wrong.

I do not think of a *relationship* when it comes to River.

She loathes me, and we could never be anything more.

I bet the sex would be explosive though...

Nolan sighs, plucking some cash from his wallet and tossing it down onto the counter. He slips his credit card back in. "Look, dude, I have listened to you lament the state of your love life since things went to shit with your ex and you got back into the dating scene, going on about how no woman has challenged you, made you feel excited for more than just bedroom activities—though why you're looking for that shit is beyond me. Hey, whatever floats your boat." He shakes his head. "Anyway, all I'm saying is, River challenges you, and there's no denying it. If you're not already entertaining the idea of a relationship with her—something I highly fucking doubt—maybe you should."

He's right. The biggest hindrance in my dating life *has* been that I haven't felt challenged or at ease with anyone. It's all the same shit, different date. The same unexciting variation of dinner, movie, bed. Rinse and fucking repeat.

It's not fun anymore. There's no chase. No excitement.

So, I guess I can see Nolan's point about River.

She is fun, and she does challenge me—mostly to not commit a crime, but it's a challenge nonetheless.

But still...she's River.

He claps me on the shoulder, giving me a small smile. "I'll call you later, man."

I nod, and he takes off.

I'm left sitting here thinking about all the ways River could be right for me...maybe in more ways than just the bedroom.

Chapter 9

RIVER

"HEY, Maya, it's River. Your boss and best friend." I add that part just so she doesn't hate me for bothering her again. "I sent you a text about this, but I'm calling too, because, well, you know me—I'm neurotic and obsessive. The meeting with the photographer got pushed tomorrow because she has to take her kid to the doctor. It's at ten now, not nine. I—"

My words die as the bedroom door is pushed open and Dean walks over the threshold.

He's drenched in sweat.

Every inch of his light blue workout shirt is clinging to him like a second skin.

I know Dean works out, not just because he's been living here five days now and he always leaves the house at the same time each night to hit the gym, but because it's obvious even through those button-up shirts and band tees he always wears.

What I wasn't expecting was to be able to *count* his abs—all six of the mouthwatering things.

He pulls his wireless headphones from his ears, the muscles in his arms jumping with the action. He's still breathing hard like he just ran all the way here from the gym.

To be honest, I wouldn't put it past him. He seems like the show-off type.

A pair of gym shorts are riding low on his hips and—

Wow. Yes. That is definitely *the outline of his dick.*

He clears his throat, and I snap my eyes to his and away from this gift he's unknowingly given me.

His dark brows are lifted, a playful smile strung across his mouth.

Busted.

"Like what you see, River?"

His words are teasing, fun.

But his eyes? The way they're burning with intensity?

They say something else entirely.

I pretend he's not staring at me like he wishes there weren't so much distance between us and pull the phone from my ear, mashing the red button on the screen. I make a mental note to explain the voicemail to Maya later and turn my nose up at Dean, forcing my attention back to the computer in front of me like I wasn't just ogling him like I've never ogled before.

"I've seen better," I say as coolly as I can muster.

I hear the waver in my own voice.

I like what I see.

I like what I see *way* more than I should.

"Sure you have. One of all those hot dates you've had?"

I hold back my sigh. Sometimes I forget he's had a front-row seat to my various dating mishaps. Living next door, I'm sure he's seen all the times I've come home alone and all the mornings I've crawled out of bed looking like a hot mess, trying to pick up my wounded heart/ego.

He laughs drily. "Please tell me it wasn't that guy wearing the Hawaiian shirt. That's going to sting."

Ah, yes. Hawaiian shirt guy.

The first date we went on was to the bowling alley. I dismissed his outfit because I thought he was being quirky. He cracked a couple jokes and the evening wasn't a complete disaster, so I said yes to a second date. This was back when I was just getting into the dating scene again and was still optimistic.

Silly me.

I let him pick me up for the second date, and imagine my surprise when I opened my door to see he was wearing *another* Hawaiian shirt.

Now, I love clothes. I love fashion and being able to use an outfit to express yourself, but there are a few places I draw the line.

Hawaiian shirts are one of them.

Of course, because that was just my luck, Dean had to step out of the elevator as we were getting on. He had *a lot* to say the next morning at the diner.

That was the last time I let a guy pick me up from my apartment; I didn't need Dean's commentary about my dating life. I'd seen plenty of women coming and going from his place over the last year and never once made any unsolicited comments about his choices.

"As a matter of fact, it was—and he had a leg up on you too. There was an eight-pack hiding beneath those *stunning* shirts."

His eyes spark. "All I just heard was that you counted my abs."

I sure as hell did. "It was a shot in the dark."

"Shot in the dark, my ass," he mutters, moving toward his pile of things.

He drops to his haunches and starts rummaging around, looking for a change of clothes. "What are you doing in here?"

"Working."

"I'm glad you came in here when I was gone and not asleep like you've done all week. Big improvement there."

I wince. "Oops. I'll bring my—"

"Work laptop home—yeah, I've heard that before."

"I'm sorry, are you being grumpy with me?"

He pauses his movements, then sighs. "Maybe a little. It's not you." He stands, turning toward me. "Well, it is…but not completely." Another sigh, his shoulders slumping on the exhale. "It's just been a long week."

He looks worn out. Run down. Like he's running on his last leg.

"I promise to bring my laptop home."

"I'm sure you will."

"I'll text Maya and make sure she reminds me."

He grunts and sits on the edge of his air mattress.

I can't imagine that's lending any hands in the sleeping department. Dean's way too big to be sleeping on that thing, and I know it's not comfortable.

We tried to rescue his bed from his apartment, but it smelled too much like smoke to us. We weren't sure if that was just the smell burned into our nostrils or if it was toast, but we weren't taking the chance.

"What are you working on this late? The shop closed hours ago."

I click through my email one last time, making sure I haven't missed anything. "Photographer."

"You have a photographer?"

I nod. "We sell items online, started it at the beginning of the year. It's still just us three managing the shop *and* now the online sales, so it's a lot of extra work to keep it running efficiently, but it will help keep business steady when tourist season is down."

A lot of work and a lot of added stress. It's why I run in here at night to check on things. Why I'm forever going in early and why I'm always the last to leave. We're a small shop, but our online presence is growing every day and the internet is demanding as hell.

"Do Caroline and Maya know you're staying up late and taking on the brunt of the work?"

There's something in his voice that almost sounds like concern.

His worry is sweet—something I never thought I'd say when referring to Dean—but it's not needed.

At the end of the day, Making Waves is mine, and since I'm not at the point of comfortably hiring more employees or paying the ones I already have more, it's only fair for it to fall on my shoulders.

"Yes."

"And what do they have to say about it?"

"Not much."

"So, what, they just think you're that good at running a well-oiled machine from the shop and not killing yourself at night?"

"No. They know I work from home sometimes."

"Do they know how often?"

I sigh. "What difference does it make to you how much time I spend working?"

"Because it wears you out and makes you overworked and you start acting extra assy."

I lift my brows. "Did you just call me an ass?"

"*Assy*, but yes."

My lips twitch, amused. "Well then."

He doesn't look sorry, and I like that he doesn't look sorry. That he sticks to his guns. That he's not afraid to call me on my shit when I'm being a brat, which is probably often.

"Just calling it like I see it." He lifts his shoulders. "I've known you for a year now and, in that time, you've grown more and more irritable. Maybe it's time for a vacation."

I narrow my eyes at him. "Did you ever stop to think that the reason is you?"

"No. I'm a fucking angel."

"If you mean in the sense that Lucifer was once an angel, you have that right."

He snorts, diving back into his bag of belongings. "Hilarious coming from you, Little Miss Call the Landlord because my music is too loud instead of just, I don't know, knocking on my door like a normal neighbor would."

"What? I've never called Lucy on you."

He peeks at me over his shoulder, his eyes in narrowed slits. "Puh-*lease*. Don't try to act all innocent now."

"I'm serious, Dean. I have never called Lucy on you. I've wanted to *a lot* but never could bring myself to do it. Other than banging on your wall, that afternoon of the fire was the first time I acted on your obnoxiousness."

He stares at me, thick brows lifted.

They slowly drop back down as the realization that I'm not lying hits him.

Does he think I'm that petty? That I'd snitch to our building manager over his music being too loud?

Have I wanted to complain to Lucy about his loud music and generally insufferable behavior? Hell yes. Every damn day.

But it wasn't me.

"Then who did?"

"Not sure, but I'd love to meet them and shake their hand. Your music taste sucks."

"You can't say that if you don't like music." Shaking his head, he pushes to his feet again, stretches his arms back over his head, and strips his shirt off in one swift movement.

My jaw drops just as easily as his clothes slid off.

He's standing not ten feet away from me without a shirt on and *oh my sweet baby Jesus.*

If I thought his body was impressive when it was covered, I was wrong. Dean's back is nothing but corded muscles, the lines defined and sexy.

Since when do I find backs sexy?

As if he knows him being shirtless is doing a number on me, he chuckles. "I can feel you staring, River."

I'm sorry, do you own a mirror? Of course I'm staring!

I gulp and give myself a good shake, turning my attention back to my computer.

Don't look, don't look, don't look.

"Weird, because I definitely wasn't staring."

Another laugh. "Just admit you find me tempting."

I wrinkle my nose and push to my feet, grabbing my

notebook. "The only thing you tempt me to do is commit murder. I—"

He turns around, and for the second time tonight, he leaves me speechless.

I'm not usually one to salivate over a man with a chiseled chest but...*good gravy.*

I can still see the beads of sweat running down the contours of his well-defined abs, the muscles jumping as my eyes rake over his body like he can feel my stare caressing him.

It's clearly been way too long since I've seen a guy shirtless because my lady bits are tingling like they've never tingled before. Fuck, even my nipples are hard, for crying out loud!

"I'm sorry, were you saying something, River?"

Like they're hooked up to his voice, they tighten even more, and I clutch my notebook like it's my lifeline, covering the evidence. Big mistake because the friction is apparently just what I need, and I nearly let out a moan.

Holy hell am I sex-deprived, getting turned on by a fucking notebook. Has nothing to do with a shirtless Dean, of course.

He steps closer, and I don't back up, holding my ground.

I shove my shoulders back. "Just that I hate you."

"Really?" He takes another step. And another. He's so close I can smell the cinnamon from his gum.

Every inch of my body is on edge because all I can think about is how he's too close but too far away at the same time.

He takes one last step, then dips his head toward mine. He's not touching me, but if I weren't holding my breath, my notebook would be bumping against his chest.

"Hate me so much you're hiding your hardened nipples behind a notebook?"

The whoosh of breath leaves me in a loud groan, and I flee from the room, careful not to brush up against him.

"Something wrong, roomie?" he calls out, amusement clear in his voice. "Did something *pop up* that you want to talk about?"

"You leave my nipples out of this!"

His laughter echoes through the apartment as I slam my bedroom door closed.

Asshole.

I CAN'T SLEEP.

I've spent the past hour tossing and turning, and it's entirely Dean's fault.

It didn't take long for him to hit the shower after I scurried off to my room. The entire time he was in there, all I could think about was how he was stark naked with nothing but a few feet of drywall between us.

How good the water must look running over his back...his abs.

His cock.

I should have been more embarrassed than I was when he caught me staring at his dick. Should have turned beet red.

But his eyes...

For a quick moment, like the *tiniest fraction* of a second, I considered closing the distance like his eyes were begging me to do.

But I didn't.

Now I'm tucked safely away in my room where I won't be tempted to do something foolish like kiss Dean Evans.

And he's in his room, where I'm sure he's just so damn pleased with himself for getting me all worked up and making my nipples hard.

They still are.

Hell, my entire body is awake because every time I close my eyes, I see Dean without a shirt. Or the outline of his dick.

Ugh. I seriously need to get laid. This is getting ridiculous if I'm actually lying here thinking about Dean of all people.

Maybe a quick rendezvous with my favorite toy will help take the edge off…

I reach into my nightstand and grab my clit vibrator. Switch it on. Set it to the lowest (and quietest) setting, slide my panties to the side.

I am *that* needy. So keyed up I nearly burst before it even makes contact with my center.

I spread my legs and tilt my hips up, guiding the toy over my bud, which is pulsing with need.

My eyes fall closed and all I see is a familiar pair of green eyes.

I pop my eyes back open, pulling the toy from my body, because *What the hell?*

It's one thing to masturbate, but it's another to think of Dean while I do it.

What he doesn't know won't hurt…

I close my eyes, bring my toy back to my clit…and god help me, I think of Dean.

His green eyes. That perfect smirk. His midnight black hair, his incessant five o'clock shadow, the slight dimple in his chin.

I conjure the image of him from only an hour ago, standing shirtless in front of me. I picture him stalking toward me, his hard, taut body pressing against mine as he cups my face. His thumb strokes gently over my cheek as he leans down to kiss me and...

I come.

Hard.

I gasp for air, coming down from the high, my heart racing dangerously fast.

"Take that, Dean." I slide the toy out from under the blankets. "I don't need the real you."

"You say something?"

"FUCK!" I yelp.

And my vibrator goes flying across the room as my arms flail.

Thump.

It smacks loudly against the wall...and leaves a nice *I was just caught masturbating and I panicked and flung my vibrator across the room*–sized hole in the wall.

"Mother..."

"Uh, everything okay in there?" Dean calls through the door.

"OH MY GOSH! GO AWAY!"

"Geez, okay," he says. "I heard talking and thought you said my name. Sorry."

His footsteps echo down the hall as I lie there, holding my breath, completely mortified. I place my hand over my chest, trying to calm my breathing. If I thought my heart rate was up during my orgasm...

What in the hell just happened?

After a few minutes of trying to relax, I push myself up to

a sitting position, combing back my hair. I smack my lips together, my mouth dry.

I drag myself out of bed and pick up my poor vibrator.

"Sorry about that, buddy," I whisper, tucking it back into my bedside table.

I quietly pull my bedroom door open. Before I step into the hallway, I peek around the doorframe and to my left.

Dean's door is closed, and his light is off.

Good.

I sneak down the hall and into the kitchen. As quietly as I can, I get myself a glass of water and chug it. I fill another and settle my back against the counter, trying to get myself to relax.

I'm even more keyed up now than I was before my stellar orgasm.

Of course Dean would ruin my afterglow. That's just his style, just the thing he'd manage to pull off, the ass.

Out of the corner of my eye, I spot my yoga mat rolled up and resting against the couch.

Yes! That's exactly what I need. Yoga always helps me cool off.

I tiptoe back to my room, grab my phone and earbuds, and then pad back out to the living room.

I unroll my mat and get everything situated before firing up my favorite yogi app.

Before I hit play, I sit still, listening closely to see if I woke Dean up with all my moving about.

Nothing.

He must be asleep.

I take a few gentle breaths and hit play on my go-to routine.

It doesn't take long until I'm lost in the moves, completely zeroed in on my favorite instructor's soothing tone.

When the video ends, I continue through my cooldown poses, determined to get out the last of the jitters I feel.

A tickle in my spine draws me out of my trance.

I'm not alone.

Dean's watching me.

His smoldering stare is boring into me. I don't have to be looking at him to know that the look in his eyes is the same one I saw earlier in his bedroom.

He's enjoying the view.

And I'm enjoying the way his eyes are caressing me, following every move I make as I bend, placing my palms flat against the floor.

Even with my headphones in, I can hear Dean's sharp intake, my ass fully on display.

I'm wearing nothing but a pair of black boyshorts and a pale pink camisole, my standard bedtime attire.

I push to my full height, then bend again, this time walking my hands out and shoving my butt out even more.

"Fuck," he mutters, the desire in his voice thick.

I can't even laugh.

I feel it too, the untapped tension in the room.

I'm starting to sweat, and not from my exercise.

The flames of his stare lick against my skin, and I realize now that screwing with him was a mistake.

I don't feel relaxed. I am anything *but* relaxed.

Inhale, exhale.

I draw in three deep breaths, stretch out again without the intention of making Dean crazy, and then push to my full height.

I don't acknowledge him as I roll my yoga mat back up and tuck it away.

Pulling one earbud from my ear, I turn toward my audience.

He doesn't look away. Doesn't shrink under my attention.

He's staring at me unabashedly, a glass of water in his hands, the moonlight from the open window and the terrarium casting just enough light for me to see him sitting at the island in the dark kitchen.

I can't see his eyes, but I can still feel them.

Feeling brave, I stalk toward him, not stopping until I'm nearly between his spread legs.

I slip the glass from his hands and take a long, hard pull from it, emptying it before setting it down on the counter.

He just watches, not saying a word as I stand there.

All that can be heard is our uneven breathing.

I don't know how many minutes go by, but my nipples are back to standing at attention and my pussy is back to feeling like I haven't given it attention in days.

I'm beginning to grow uncomfortable under his deep stare, and not in a creeper vibe sort of way. More of an *I'm about to do something I regret* kind of way.

"Like what you see?" I smart off, needing to regain some semblance of balance because what in the hell are we doing?

We can't be playing games like this.

I can't be masturbating because Dean got me all hot and bothered.

He can't be staring at me like he wants to strip me bare.

"Yes," he answers.

Without a care in the world, he adjusts his obviously hard cock inside those gray sweats I'm starting to hate.

"Yeah?"

A challenging brow goes up.

"Well, that's too bad."

Though I want to run, I turn away from him slowly, sauntering down the hall as nonchalantly as I can.

"Fucking hell," he grumbles as I close my door.

Fucking hell is right.

Chapter 10

DEAN

"WHAT THE HELL are you staring at?"

The fluff of white fur bores his bright blue, hate-filled gaze into me from the other end of the couch where I've been planted all day.

Morris does not like me one bit. He made that clear last night when I got up to use the bathroom and he swatted at me as I made my way down the hall. I'm now sporting two slashes across the top of my left foot that I know will sting later when I put my shoes on for my nightly visit to the gym.

With an annoyed *meow*, the little shithead picks himself up and saunters off down the hallway, leaving me to enjoy bumming around without being watched.

I look over at Leo, and I swear he rolls his eyes at Morris.

"Same, dude. Same." I reach over, running my finger along the glass of his terrarium.

He looks as tired as I feel.

It's not often I take days to just lounge around. I'm not an overly busy man by any means, but I always tend to find *something* to do to fill my time, like signing up for summer school or my volunteer work with the local animal shelter where I got Leo. Sitting still isn't my thing.

But today, I needed it.

It's been a long week, and I've been in constant go mode

dealing with insurance, Lucy—who I swear is an angel—and the aftermath of nearly burning my own place down.

Shit, I've been so busy I forgot to tell my parents about the fire and received a nice phone call from my mother this morning that consisted of a whole lot of swearing and promises of *I brought you into this world, Dean Evans, and I can take you out.*

I can thank Holland's big mouth for spilling those beans.

After that horrid wake-up call, I decided a day of doing nothing sounded perfectly acceptable. Especially since I didn't sleep for shit last night.

I couldn't stop thinking about River...or how she looked bent over. How she looked practically standing between my legs with nipples as hard as rocks.

I had to fight so fucking hard to not reach out and touch her.

Just like I've had to fight hard today to talk myself out of stroking my cock to the image of her ass in the air.

I should be ashamed of myself for conjuring it up so many times, but I refuse. Not when she looked as good as she did.

Stop thinking about it, Dean. It's a bad idea to go there.

I focus my attention back on the guitar in my hands, plucking at the strings. I'm not the best guitarist there is and I don't play often, but it's a good distraction when I'm trying to relax.

Keys slip into the lock on the front door, and Morris races back into the living room, perching by the door just as River pushes it open.

"Hi, baby." She coos at him like he isn't the devil in disguise, trading the purse in her hands for him, swooping the cat up and cuddling him close. I can hear his purring all the way from the couch as she scratches under his ears, peppering him with kisses.

Like she can feel my gaze, she turns her eyes to me.

"Oh. Hi."

Her voice might be flat, but there's something different in the way she's looking at me. I can't quite put my finger on what I'm seeing.

"How was your day?" I ask.

She scrunches her face up. "Can you not?"

"Can I not what? Be civil?"

"Be domestic. It's weird."

"Right." I nod. "My bad. I'll skip the pleasantries next time and just rip ass as soon as you walk through the door."

Her eyes widen. "You've been farting on my couch?"

I don't even dignify that with a response.

Instead, I push up from my spot of comfort and set my guitar to the side. I pick up my water glass and make my way into the kitchen to deposit it in the sink.

She sighs. "Sorry. That probably wasn't an appropriate response."

Now I'm the one with wide eyes as I turn to her. "Did you just...apologize? To *me*?"

She wants to roll her eyes. It's all over her face. Somehow, she refrains, settling for a poorly repressed sigh as she sets Morris down on the floor. He meows at her, then prances off, heading to his bed beside the TV stand.

River slides her shoes off, then pads farther into the apartment. "Don't get too excited. I also apologized to the potted plant I ran into in the hallway. You're not special." She slips onto the stool at the counter. "Might want to pay attention."

I pinch my brows together. "Huh?"

She nods toward the glass that's under the water spigot on the fridge just as it begins to overflow onto my hand.

"Shit!" I yank it away, and it's a foolish thing to do. Water sloshes everywhere.

I take one step, and my least favorite thing in the world happens: I step in water...with my socks on.

"Son of a bitch!"

River giggles.

Actually *giggles*.

I whip my head toward her. I've never heard a sound like that come out of her before.

If she's laughing when I'm around, it's at me, and it can mostly be classified as more of a sarcastic snort than anything else.

"You sounded like Dean."

"I am Dean."

This time she does roll her eyes. "Not *you* Dean. Winchester. The one I actually like."

"You know, me and that Dean have a lot in common. It's weird you don't like me too."

"I'm sorry, have you *seen* Jensen Ackles without a shirt on?"

"Have you seen *me* without a shirt on?"

She purses her lips. "You know I have."

"And?"

She swallows thickly, the action visible even from here, and wiggles in her seat.

She clears her throat and waves her hand, trying to appear unaffected. "Not impressed."

"That's not what your nipples said." I lift my leg, pulling

my wet sock off my foot, then remove the other. I ball them up and shove them into my pocket.

If I were in my own place, I'd toss them on the floor.

I have a feeling that wouldn't go over too well with River.

"There was a draft."

"In a bedroom with all the windows closed?"

"Yes," she says. Then she points across the kitchen. "Second drawer, next to the stove."

"What?"

She huffs. "Hand towels. Second drawer down, next to the stove. You're going to need them to clean your mess up. I don't have paper towels."

"Did you forget to buy some?"

"No. I just don't use them at home. Reuse, reduce, recycle and all that. I try to do my part where I can, and paper towels seem pointless when there are perfectly good washable cloth napkins and towels that can be used."

"That's...surprising."

"What is?"

"You being all hipster and whatnot."

"If *being all hipster* means giving a shit about the environment, then yeah, I guess I am a 'hipster.'" She uses air quotes around the word. "Do you need assistance?"

"Are you going to keep talking like that all night?"

"Like what?"

"Just throwing out these random questions like I'm supposed to know what the hell you're yammering on about."

"I'm referring to your mess. Do you need help cleaning it up? It's taking you long enough to do it."

I shake my head, moving toward the drawer she pointed out, and clean up my mess.

River rises from her stool, moving into the kitchen, stepping around me and having the audacity to side-eye me like *I'm* the one in *her* way.

Finished cleaning, I stand to my full height, tossing the towel onto the counter next to me. I lean my back against the granite and cross my arms over my chest, watching as she scuttles around, peeking in all the cabinets and shuffling things around before slamming them closed.

"Are you hangry or something? Need a snack? You sound extra grumpy today."

"Yes, actually." She pulls the door of the fridge/freezer open, and it takes all of five seconds before she angrily bangs it closed too. "I'm *starving*, and there's nothing to eat in this apartment."

"Didn't we just go grocery shopping?"

"Yes, but nothing sounds good."

Truth is, I'm also starving, and now that we're bringing up food, my stomach is starting to rumble. I did this same routine three times today before I settled on eating a couple spoonfuls of peanut butter straight from the jar that was clearly marked with…well, not my name.

But I'm not telling her that.

"Let's go out."

She crinkles her nose. "Like…together? In…public?"

I pin her with a narrowed stare. "Yes."

"Where people can see us?"

"River…" I pinch the bridge of my nose between my thumb and forefinger.

"Fine, fine," she relents. "We can go to The Gravy Train. People already know us there, so it won't be weird if we're seen together."

"You're acting like I'm some sort of leper."

"You said it, not me."

I shove away from the counter, brushing past her. "I'll go get dressed."

"You mean you're not going to wear such an orgasm-inducing outfit out and about?"

I spin back around. "You know what? Yeah, I think I will. I mean, you go to the diner looking like shit on a log all the time. Why can't I?"

She works her jaw back and forth at my lie.

River might not always be dressed up, but she certainly never looks like shit, even when she's trying to.

"Whatever." She breezes past me, making her way to the front door. "Just don't stand too close to me."

"Oh, I'm standing close—super close. I might even hold your hand just so everyone knows we're together."

"Please." She slips her shoes back on as I stalk toward her, swiping my wallet and phone from the coffee table and stuffing them into my pocket. "Like they'd believe that. We hate each other. Everyone knows it."

"Good point. You're not very subtle about your distaste for me."

"Can you blame me?" she shoots back, grabbing her purse as I pull open the front door and wave her through. "You first. I have the key."

"Which I *still* need a copy of," I remind her as I head into the hall. I've asked her every morning *and* night since I moved in and she's yet to get me a copy.

"So you've said about ten times. It's on my to-do list."

"Where? At the very bottom?"

Her grin tells me I'm right.

Before she can pull the door shut all the way, I reach into my pocket, grab the ball of wet socks, and chuck them into the apartment.

"Dean!"

"What?" I say innocently. "I'll pick 'em up when we get back. I wasn't going to go to The Gravy Train with wet socks in my pocket."

"But you'll bring your turtle there?"

"He's my emotional support turtle!"

"Sure he is." She turns the lock and I trail behind her toward the elevator, loving the way her ass looks in the skintight jeans she's rocking. "And Michael B. Jordan proposed to me today."

"That poor, poor bastard."

She smacks at my stomach. "I hope Morris steals your socks and hides them where you'll never find them."

"And I hope Michael B. Jordan did propose—it'd be nice for someone to finally take you off my hands."

"That implies you have some sort of hold on me, and I can assure you that couldn't be further from the truth."

"Couldn't it though?" I smirk as we wait for the elevator. "You seem pretty obsessed with me."

"You wish."

The elevator arrives and the doors open to show another building resident tucked inside, standing at the back corner.

I don't remember the woman's name—something with a T —but she smiles at us warmly as we step into the car and stand opposite her.

The ride is quiet as we make our way down ten floors.

When the car hits the lobby, she grins at us brightly as she steps out of the elevator. "I always knew you two would get together eventually."

"What the fuck..." I whisper once she's out of earshot.

"For once, I agree with you," River says. She wrinkles her nose as we make our way off the elevator. "Do people, like, think we're...dating?" She shivers, pushing through the building's main doors. "Ew."

I prickle at her reaction.

She hates me, I get it, but to imply that dating me would be gross grates on me for some reason.

"Ouch."

"Don't act like that hurt your feelings. You know us dating would be awful."

"Eh."

"I'm sorry, are you implying us dating *wouldn't* be a disaster?"

"It could be good. Especially for your reputation."

She chortles. "Please. If anything, it would be quite the opposite."

"What was it you said to me before?" I scratch my chin. "Ah, that's right—whatever you need to tell yourself to help you sleep in the room across from me at night."

She lifts her eyes skyward.

"Careful," I tell her. "You keep rolling your eyes like that and they'll get stuck that way."

She does it again, with extra flair this time.

I chuckle, grabbing hold of the door to The Gravy Train and pulling it open for her. She doesn't move away as my fingers brush against the small of her back to guide her into the restaurant.

We file into the line, and there are at least five people ahead of us. River isn't happy about it.

"I swear, if someone takes the last piece of cherry pie, I'm going to be *big mad*." She's standing there with her arms crossed over her chest, tapping her foot against the old, worn black and white checkered tile. She looks ticked off, and it's adorable how bothered she's getting. "Like the biggest kind of mad a person can get. Flipping tables and everything."

"You take your pie seriously when you're hungry."

"I take my pie seriously all the time." She side-eyes me as we step forward. "Something you should remember the next time you want to try to steal it."

"Is it stealing if it's given to me?"

"Considering you trick a poor, unsuspecting *child* into 'giving' it to you, yes—that's stealing."

I laugh. "Man, that kid is gullible. Maya should work on that."

A proud smile curves River's lips. "She's a good mom."

"She is." I nod. "I see a lot of parents come through my classroom who aren't. Makes me realize that even when I thought I had it bad as a kid, it could have been worse."

"Where are you from originally?"

"Not too far away. About an hour and a half south."

"Why'd you move up here?"

I turn to her, surprised. "I'm sorry, are you trying to *get to know me* or something?"

"Not really. I'm just trying to distract myself from the hunger that's ripping through my stomach so I don't skip this ridiculous line and start stealing treats right off the counter."

"There are three people in front of us now. The line isn't *that* ridiculous."

She shrugs, and we move up again.

"Now two."

She growls, and I laugh.

Pushing to her toes, she bobs side to side, trying to see what's going on in front of her, her patience wearing thin as the old couple at the counter—who I'm fairly certain were around when the dinosaurs were—move slowly.

Her legs look long encased in her skinny jeans, and I know it's an optical illusion because she barely comes up to my shoulders on a good day.

The mustard and black polka dot shirt she's wearing rides up at her movements, giving me a peek at her skin.

And now all I can think about is last night.

How good she looked in the moonlight doing whatever fucking pose she was doing. She could have been down there making shit up completely and I wouldn't have known. I'd have watched her all night if I could.

The last of the line in front of us disappears and we step up to the register.

The woman behind the counter blinks twice, clearly surprised to see us.

"River. Dean. You're here...together?" She phrases it as a question, her curious eyes darting between us.

"Yep." I smile at her. "Just grabbing some dinner, Darlene."

"Together?"

I try to hide my laugh, but it's difficult, especially when I can feel the annoyance coming off River in waves.

"Yes. Together. May I please have a coffee and a slice of cherry first, then a Don't Go Bacon My Heart."

"I'm sorry, River, but you just missed the last of the cherry."

Her hazel eyes fill with fury.

Uh-oh.

"What?"

The word is clipped, and even Darlene takes a step back.

"T-Terribly sorry, dear. We sold out just a few minutes ago."

"But it's Saturday night! You always have cherry pie on Saturday nights. Everyone's so ecstatic for pecan day that the cherry slips under the radar." River's eyes fall to slits. "It was that dinosaur man, wasn't it?"

Darlene doesn't answer, but the thick swallow is telling enough.

"I knew it!" River explodes. "That's it. I'm going after him."

She takes two steps before I'm wrapping my arm around her waist, holding her in place.

"What are you going to do? Go steal a slice of pie from an old man?"

"Yes!" She squirms in my grasp, trying to free herself to go do just that.

The saddest part is, I believe her.

She's desperate at this point.

"You cannot steal pie from customers, River, especially not the old ones. That man is easily in his nineties. For all you know, this could be his last piece of pie ever."

"It could be mine too!" She tries to run again, and I grip her tighter.

Big mistake.

The friction she's causing is making my already lonely

cock weep with the little attention it's receiving. If she doesn't stop, it's going to be obvious that I'm enjoying having her rubbing against me way too much.

Knowing River, I doubt I'd skate through that embarrassment unscathed.

I drop my lips to her ear. "Remember what your little yoga show did to me last night? I didn't even touch you, and you did that to me. Do you want to be writhing against me right now?"

Like I knew it would, it works, and she stops fighting me.

I relax my hold on her but don't fully let her go, not trusting her one bit.

Her cheeks are red as she straightens, smoothing down her shirt. "You can let me go now, Dean."

I don't.

"Can I trust you?" I say, my lips a little too close to her ear.

"Yes."

"Do you promise not to chase after a poor, helpless old man and behave?"

She grunts. "Yes."

"Okay." Slowly, I release my hold on her and take a step back, letting out a relieved breath because I could *really* use the space.

If she noticed anything rubbing against her, she keeps it to herself, not saying anything as she adjusts her clothes and sorts herself out.

"Now, go get us a table while I finish ordering."

"Fine, but only because if I leave, you'll have to pay for my dinner."

She takes off in the direction of where the old man went and I grab her wrist, tugging her back toward me.

I shake my head as she peeks up at me innocently.

"The *other* way," I tell her.

She pouts and doesn't like it but does what I tell her, sashaying off to find us a seat on the other side of the diner.

When she's out of earshot, I turn my attention back to the register.

"Sorry about that, Darlene."

She's sporting a lopsided grin, shaking her head at me.

"What?" I ask.

"Oh, boy. You have it *bad* for her."

I pull my brows together and decide to ignore her preposterous comment. "I'll take a coffee and a Couldn't If I Fried."

She sniggers. "Of course that's what you want."

"What?"

"It just makes sense considering River ordered the—"

"Don't Go Bacon My Heart," I finish. "Okay, I got it, but you're reading too much into it. I always order the Couldn't If I Fried."

"And she always orders the bacon."

She does?

Whatever. So what if we always order meals with ludicrously cutesy names that sound like they go together? Doesn't mean a damn thing.

"Listen, if I slip you an extra ten, can you tell that guy who ordered the cherry pie it fell on the floor and sneak it over to my table?"

That goofy grin that hasn't left her face grows. "For River? Or for you?"

"Darlene…"

She laughs. "Make it twenty and you got yourself a deal, sugar."

I pay for our meals—plus the extra bribe—and make my way over to the table River grabbed us.

She's sitting there fuming, shooting daggers across the diner at the old man, practically staring a hole in his back.

"Leave him be, River."

"He stole my pie, Dean, and you *always* steal my pie. People are always stealing my damn pie and it's totally not cool."

"You could try getting here earlier, you know. Then maybe you'd have a chance at getting your precious pie."

"You say that like I'm the only one of us who likes pie." She gasps, eyes wide. "Holy shit. I swear if you're just buying up all the pie because you know I like it and you don't even truly love it and adore it like it's meant to be loved and adored, I'm going to murder you. No, first I'll kick you out of my apartment, and then I'll murder you."

"Well, that's doubly awful of you."

"And true."

She picks her fork up off the table, holding it toward me in what she thinks is a threatening manner, but I'm certain this is what being threatened by a grumpy, hungry toddler is like.

"Relax, turbo," I say, snatching the fork away from her. "I truly love and adore the pie in just the way it's meant to be loved and adored."

She lets out a relieved breath, sitting back into the booth. "Good. Because I'd hate to have to murder you."

"Developing a soft spot for me, huh?"

"No. I just don't want to get blood all over my shoes. They're my favorite."

I laugh. "Fair enough."

"Here are those coffees." Darlene sets a cup in front of each of us. "And I found this for you, River."

She winks at her as she slides over a plate with a single piece of cherry pie on it, then scurries away.

River's entire face lights up, and something in my chest shifts. I don't know what exactly. All I know is that was the best twenty bucks I've spent all week.

She moves faster than I've ever seen her, snatching her fork back and stabbing into the pie, shoving a bite far larger than she can handle into her mouth.

She moans, and there goes my dick jumping to attention again.

I shift in my seat, attempting to adjust my aching cock without making what I'm doing too obvious.

I don't think I've ever seen her this happy before, and that includes the time she thought she saw Hugh Jackman walk by the diner.

She even *smiles at me.*

And I find myself smiling back.

"This is the best thing to happen to me all week."

"What? Having dinner with me?"

Her smile wanes but doesn't disappear. "If having dinner with you means free pie, then yes. Though I do wonder how Darlene managed to scrounge this up..."

Her words trail off as she tilts her head, studying me.

"What?" I fidget under her inspection.

"Did you have something to do with this?"

"What? No." But my voice sounds too high even to my own ears. I clear my throat. "Of course not."

"Developing a soft spot for me, Dean?" she asks with a smirk, tossing my words back at me.

Maybe.

I roll my eyes. "Just shut up and eat your pie, River."

She does, and she doesn't stop grinning at me the entire time.

That odd feeling in my chest lingers.

Chapter 11

RIVER

"DID you know you're out of eggs?"

I narrow my eyes at Dean as he walks into the living room, shoving a forkful of food into his gob. "Why are you counting my eggs?"

A shit-eating grin stretches across his mouth, and I'm annoyed by how good he looks even though he has a piece of egg stuck to his lip. "Because I don't want you to starve. I remember two nights ago when you tried to maim an old man for stealing your pie quite well, and I'd like to avoid a repeat."

Okay, so maybe I was a little temperamental the other night.

But it was entirely Dean's fault.

He was the one who got me so worked up I couldn't *not* take care of myself, which of course led to mayhem and a late-night workout.

Dean's eyes roaming over me during my impromptu yoga session had me more awake than ever, and I didn't fall asleep until nearly sunrise. When I finally peeled myself out of bed the next morning and saw the hole my toy left in the wall, I knew I couldn't face Dean.

I hightailed it to Making Waves even though it was my

day off, skipping breakfast so I didn't have to risk an unwanted run-in with my roomie. My entire day was off-kilter after that.

Like I said, completely his fault.

"I highly doubt you're concerned about my eating habits." I hold my coffee up to my lips and blow on the hot liquid.

It doesn't take a genius to know he's been sneaking my eggs and nearly all the other food in the fridge and pantry that's labeled mine. It's like the rules we carefully drew mean absolutely nothing to him.

He beams at me as he plops down onto the other end of the couch. It's that same damn smile he's been giving me since he moved in, like he knows having him here is killing me.

And it is.

Mentally…physically.

I'm wound tight. Tighter than usual, that's for damn sure. Having him around is stressing me out. Relaxation is a thing of the past. And I don't just mean the "chilling with no pants on" or "letting my titties fly free" kind—that's a whole different level of leisure.

I mean just sitting on my own couch and watching crappy television. Or walking into my own kitchen and eating a pint of ice cream without feeling his judgment bore into me. Even simply existing in my own space and not feeling on edge or like a guest in my own apartment. Don't even get me started on the way he regularly pads around this place like he is now, dressed in those panty-dropping gray sweats and a plain white t-shirt like he's some sex god.

I hate every moment of it.

Especially at night when I lie in bed thinking about the

fact that Dean Fucking Evans is lying across the hall…and how good it might feel to cross the threshold of his room and curl into bed next to him. To let him touch me with his hands the way he did with his eyes.

To kiss him.

"Thank you for the inventory," I tell him. "I'll mark that down for the next time we do our grocery shopping…and you'll take note of the carefully crafted plan we laid out."

I give him a short smile, letting him know I'm not taking any more of his shit, including him stealing my food.

He laughs.

He has the fucking audacity to *laugh.*

"You mean writing our names on our crap like we're in kindergarten or something? Come on, River. It's not a big deal if we use each other's things. I know you use some of my stuff."

"I don't use anything of yours."

He raises his brows, and I work overtime to not let my shoulders drop.

Shit. He knows.

To be fair, it's his fault I use his things. He just smells *so damn good.* Like so good I want to bathe in his scent…

So, I do.

I might have started using his bodywash in the shower.

But can I really be blamed? That cedar scent flowing over me…damn. It almost makes me feel not so single and lonely when I use it.

Sad, but true.

"I don't," I repeat, maintaining my composure.

He gives me a look like he doesn't believe me but drops it anyway.

"So," he starts, pushing his food around and mixing it up. "What's on your agenda today?"

Luckily, since Dean has lived here, I've been distracted by work. I've made sure to leave early each day and stay late each night just to avoid extra time with him.

Rude? Yes.

Necessary so I don't commit murder? Also yes.

I'm sure I could conjure *something* up and sneak off to the shop, but I could use a day away.

I love Making Waves—it's my baby—but even I need a breather every so often, and this week has been extra hard. I could use a break.

Besides, I have a feeling after showing up to the shop yesterday when I wasn't supposed to be there, if Caroline and Maya found out I did it again…well, let's just say facing their wrath isn't on my list of things I want to do anytime soon.

"For the first time in a long time, not a damn thing. Do you work?"

He shakes his head. "Summer school doesn't start until next week."

"Anything to take care of with the apartment?"

"Stalemate with insurance."

"You'll be home today, then?"

He nods. "Yep."

"Oh."

He takes a bite of whatever it is of mine he's eating, chews, and swallows. "Do you want me to get out of your hair after breakfast so you can have the place to yourself?"

And there he goes making me like him just a little bit more again.

Would it make my life easier if I didn't have him hanging

around all the time and was able to truly relax in my own house? Yes.

But am I going to kick him out for the day when he's already going through all the shit he's going through? No.

He might be the world's most obnoxious person, but I'm not cruel.

He stretches his legs out, placing his feet on the coffee table. I reach over and smack at them, but he disregards me, leaving them where they are.

Morris, who's hiding under the table, snakes his paw out and swats at him, backing me up.

"Son of a..." Dean yanks his feet down, taking the not-so-subtle hint.

He glowers at Morris as he climbs into my lap, curling into a ball and purring.

"Why would you ask that?"

"Just that I had a lazy-fest the other day myself. I bet you could use one too."

"Are you saying I'm wound tight?"

"Given that you were up doing yoga at midnight the other night, yes." He peeks over at me with a coy smile. "Unless you weren't up because you're stressed and it was something else entirely."

Not coy. Sinister.

For a split second, I forgot Dean is the devil in disguise.

"I don't do well with sitting still," I tell him. "*That's* why I was up doing yoga." *Partial lie.* "It had nothing to do with anything else."

"I'm not good about sitting still either. It's why I sign up for summer school every year and spend so many hours at the shelter."

"Shelter?"

He jerks his thumb over his shoulder. "Where I got this shithead."

Leo, who's lazing away on a bed of rocks, lifts his head, and I swear he makes direct eye contact with me like he knows we're talking about him.

"You weren't kidding about him being your emotional support turtle?"

"I'm *his* emotional support handler. And, no. Why would I lie about that?"

"Because it's weird."

"Because he's a turtle?"

"Yes." I take another careful sip of my coffee. "It wouldn't be as weird if it was like, I don't know, a cat or something."

"Nah." Dean shakes his head. "I hate cats."

"Hey!" I point to my lap. "Morris can hear you!"

"I said what I said, Morris."

Meow.

"Pretty sure that means *Feeling's mutual* in cat."

He chuckles. "You're probably right."

"What made you get an emotional support turtle?" Dean opens his mouth to correct me, and I roll my eyes. "You know what I mean."

"I wish I had a good story, but I was just walking by the shelter not long after I moved here and saw a sign that said *Volunteers Needed.* I didn't know anyone in town yet and still had time before school started, so I figured why not? I had nothing better to do." His tone is casual, but the way he glances over at Leo with a smile on his lips tells a different story. "About a week into volunteering, this little guy was brought in. He was wild captured and taken care of for a couple of years before he was accidentally run over by one of those big Power Wheels cars. His shell was badly cracked, and the family didn't want to fix him, so they surrendered him to the shelter. Luckily, he was able to be patched back up, but it can take a long time for a shell to heal. I felt awful for him. He's a turtle, you know? Not some fluffy cat or chubby little puppy. Nobody was going to give him the time of day. So, I took him home. He's been with me since."

He puts his hand up to the terrarium and Leo makes his way over to the glass, tapping his head against where Dean's palm is like they've done it a million times before.

My heart melts.

He pulls his hand away, putting his attention back on his plate. "Anyway, I'm not able to go as often during the school year because I'm so busy, but I try to dedicate at least two days a week to the shelter during the summer."

He might talk like he only walked into the shelter because he was bored, but it's clear he has a soft spot in his heart for broken things.

He looks over at me, chewing the last of his food. "What?" he asks, swallowing. "Why are you looking at me like that?"

"Nothing." I shake my head. "It's nothing."

Only it's not.

I'm starting to think Dean might not be as bad as I once thought.

Still annoying? Yes.

But maybe there's more to him than I thought…and that could be dangerous.

"You never answered me," he says.

"What did you ask?"

"Do you want me to make myself scarce in the apartment today?"

"No."

"Cool. Want to go do something fun with me, then? Something to help blow off steam and maybe help you relax?"

"SURE."

Wait...what?

Why did I say that? And why do I mean it?

"YOU'RE KIDDING."

I stare up at the red, barn-style building I've driven by many times but haven't ever been inside.

"Nope."

"*This* is what you had in mind?"

"Yep." He pulls the door open. "Come on."

"Are you serious?"

"Dead."

"Aren't we a little too old for this?"

"Are we too old to have fun? No. Now, come on."

"Why the hell not?"

With a shrug, I breeze past him into what is aptly named The Skate Barn, a roller rink.

The first thing I notice is the smell—*old*. It's not entirely unpleasant, but it smells dated for sure. The second is the décor. There are old concert posters, flyers, and tickets stapled to the walls. It's cluttered, but in an artsy sort of way.

To my surprise, the place isn't completely dead. There are

about ten people out on the floor flying around the rink, and a few stragglers in the middle moving more slowly. There's soft music playing through the speakers and a couple kids running amuck in the small game room.

"This place is…"

"Awesome!" Dean claps his hands together. "Oh, man. I haven't been in one of these in *forever*. I've seen it on my drive over the past year I've lived here but haven't had the chance to come check it out yet."

"I've never been in either. I don't think I've even set foot in one of these since I was like five."

"Really? We had one in my hometown. Throughout middle school, it was always packed on a Friday night. The hottest place to go, that's for sure."

"I take it you're a great skater, then?"

He shrugs. "I can manage. You?"

It's going to be embarrassing as hell and I am not looking forward to it. "I'll manage too."

"Good. Let's go grab some skates."

Dean places his hand on the small of my back, and my skin hums just like it did the other night when he made the same move.

It's silly. It's not like I haven't had guys do it to me before. But Dean's touch…it's different.

Firm, yet gentle. Like he's touching me because he wants to keep me safe and close and because he can't help himself.

I like it.

Dean requests skates in our sizes, then we make our way over to an empty bench and swap our shoes for the four-wheeled style.

He's laced up first, while I struggle.

"Need help?" he asks, towering above me with his hands on his hips.

I glower up at him, shoving my hair out of my face. "I'm not a child. I can tie my own skates."

"Are you sure? Because at this rate, we'll be here all day."

"You can go out without me."

He gives me a look that says he believes otherwise.

Then, he drops to his knees, and I hold still as he curls his hand around my calf.

If I thought having his hand on my lower back was making my skin vibrate before, I was wrong.

This? It's next level.

It's not like this is the first time Dean's touched me. He had me plastered against him in the diner just two nights ago, but I was too focused on food to pay attention to what it felt like to be in his arms.

If the way it feels to have his hand on my leg is any indication, I missed out big-time.

Slowly, like he can feel the difference too, he drags his hand down my calf, lifting my leg until my skate is resting against his giant thigh. His fingers move swiftly as he gets my laces straightened out.

"You should tie your hair up so it's not flying around in your face out there."

"I thought you liked my hair down?"

He peeks up at me, brow lifted. "Since when do you care about what I like?"

I don't answer him.

Instead, I do what he tells me, wrapping my long hair into a bun and securing it messily on top of my head.

He sets my now laced feet back on the floor, then hops

onto his with ease, like he was born wearing a pair of skates or something.

He reaches his hand out to me. "You ready?"

"As I'll ever be."

I let him pull me up. I truly haven't been on skates in a *long* time, probably since I was about eight or so. That time, Maya and I both decided it would be fun to try to climb the pine tree near our house in them…then proceeded to fall and scare the living shit out of our parents and ourselves. We threw our skates in the Dumpster the very next morning.

"Come on." He starts to lead us toward the floor. "I know you said it's been a long time since you've been on these, so when we get out there, I can help guide you if you need it. I'll—"

He jerks to a stop and I run right into him.

Those comedians who do the exaggerated fall with their arms flailing and their feet swishing back and forth like they can't find traction until they smack into the ground?

Yeah, that's me right now.

My legs fly out from under me and I land straight on my ass.

Dean topples over right along with me.

"Shit!" he shouts as he goes down.

The air is driven from my lungs as he lands on top of me, all ten billion pounds of muscles pressing against me.

He scrambles up, pushing himself off me until he's hovering like he's about to do a push-up or some shit. "Shit! Crap! Shit! Are you okay?"

I groan, and he peers down with concerned eyes.

"Are you okay?"

"Yes?"

It's a question because quite frankly, everything hurts.

He leans in so close I can see at least three different shades of green in his eyes.

"Please tell me you didn't hit your head."

"I didn't." He exhales, relieved. "But I'm pretty sure my tailbone is nonexistent at this point."

He laughs, closing his eyes and dropping his forehead to mine. "I can work with a broken butt, but not a concussion."

I stop breathing again.

I stop moving.

I'm pretty sure time stops too, because I couldn't tell you how long goes by as we lie here, Dean on top of me and me trying not to breathe, like I'm a corpse in a TV show and the camera is zoomed in on my face.

He sinks lower. I swear I can feel his lips ghosting against mine.

And I swear I want to feel more.

"River?"

"Yeah?"

He swallows. Once. Twice.

"I…uh…I—"

"Well, this is an interesting turn of events."

We whip our heads toward the voice coming from above.

"Hey, Lucy," Dean drawls out casually.

Our building manager stands over us, her bright purple-painted lips stretching from ear to ear, hands on her hips.

Dean rolls off me, sitting beside me, drawing his knees up. I push up to sitting, my tailbone seriously aching with the movements.

"How are you?"

Lucy tucks her lips together at Dean's ridiculous attempt to act like she didn't just catch us almost kissing.

Holy. Fucking. Shit.

Dean Evans just almost kissed me!

And I almost let him.

"What are you kids doing here?" she asks.

"Skating."

"On the floor? Horizontally?"

Dean's face turns as deep red as my hair.

Lucy laughs. "I'm only teasing, but I am glad to see it's finally happened. I always knew you two would get together."

What is it with people saying that?

Furrowing my brow, I glance at Dean, and he appears to be just as confused as I am.

He clears his throat. "What are you doing here?"

"Just getting some practice in."

"Practice?"

Lucy nods. "Roller derby."

His brows shoot into his hairline. "*You* play roller derby?"

"Used to. I was a badass, too. Lawless is what they called me, because I was awful about following the rules." She shrugs. "Now, I ref. I get to bust the balls now."

I'm sure the Lawless nickname also had a lot to do with the fact that she resembles Xena with her long black hair and blunt bangs.

"That's still pretty badass, especially for..." His words trail off, eyes growing wide as he realizes what he was about to say and how he's completely helpless to talk himself out of it.

I might be enjoying watching him squirm under Lucy's scrutiny just a bit too much.

"Someone my age?" she provides for him, tilting her head. "Just how old do you think I am, Dean?"

He swallows loudly. "I just meant…uh…I meant…"

She chuckles. "I'm only kidding. I'm aware I'm no spring chicken. Doesn't mean I can't have fun, right?"

She winks, and I wonder if she somehow overheard our earlier conversation outside because it sounds almost exactly like what Dean said to me.

"Right," he agrees quietly.

I've seen Dean be a lot of things before, but never embarrassed like he is now, staring straight down at his lap and not making eye contact with our building manager.

Lucy gives me another wink and gestures toward the rink. "See you kids out there, yeah?"

She skates off like she was born on wheels, but neither of us make a move to follow her.

"She's totally going to jack my rent up after that comment," Dean says, staring after her.

"Nah, Lucy is way too nice. Proof: you're still living in the building when you're clearly being reported consistently. That reminds me…why do you think *I'm* the one reporting you?"

"Because you live next door and I probably annoy you the most."

"That is likely one hundred percent accurate, but alas, it's truly not me."

"Why not?"

I peek over at him, and he's watching me with intense eyes. "I'm not sure."

I've wanted to report Dean for the last several months, but every time I pick up my laptop to log into the system and file a complaint, I never submit the form. I've written up at least ten over the last year. All of them end up in the trash.

I don't know what stops me.

"Is it that soft spot you're developing for me?"

Soft spot? For him? He wishes. There's no way I have anything that resembles a soft spot for him. He's the most obnoxious man on the planet. If aliens invaded Earth and we had to send a sacrifice with them to save humankind, I'd personally escort Dean onto their ship.

Then why haven't you reported him? And the better question...why were you going to let him kiss you?

"Trust me, there's no soft spot."

"Right." He chuckles, shaking his head. He pushes up to his feet with ease, then extends a hand my way. "Come on. Let's go see how bad we suck at this."

Chapter 12

DEAN

"YOU HAVE GOT to be fucking kidding me..."

I growl, tapping my head against the door and gripping the handle until my knuckles are turning white.

Locked out again.

I wish I'd have stopped in at the hardware store with her in tow and forced her to make me a key the day we went to the roller rink, but the only thing that was running through my mind was that I almost kissed her.

I almost kissed River, and if Lucy hadn't interrupted us, I would have.

Hell, even almost a week later, I'd probably *still* be kissing her.

Long. Hard. In all the ways I've thought about when I'm unable to sleep at night and unwilling to tug my cock with her in the room across the hall.

Right now, I don't want to kiss her. I'm too damn annoyed by her.

I bang on the door. "Dammit, River! Let me in!"

An older woman from across the hall steps out of her apartment, her face pinched with disapproval. She's given me similar looks before, and now that I know it's not River,

I'd bet good money *she's* the one complaining to Lucy about me.

I give her a tight smile.

"It's a sex-game thing."

She gasps, clutching her chest and hurrying faster down the hall in an effort to get away from me.

I don't feel sorry for scaring her. I'm too fucking frustrated.

I need a key to this apartment, and that changes…*now*.

I beat on the door yet again. "River! Open up, dammit!"

"Wow."

I whirl around, startled by the sound.

River's standing about three doors down, right across from the elevator. She's leaned against the wall, arms crossed, watching me with a raised brow.

"Telling old ladies we're playing sex games *and* cussing at me. And here I thought you were a gentleman, Dean."

I scoff. "You entertained no such notion." She shrugs. "Now come open the door."

"You're not technically wrong." She shoves off the wall, making her way toward me with the world's slowest gait—probably because she fell no less than ten times while roller skating. With the same snail's pace, she pulls her keys from her pocket and slips the correct one into the lock, twisting them both and pushing the door open, motioning for me to go first.

"I might be an asshole sometimes, but ladies always go first."

She grumbles something I can't make out and pushes past me. I follow her inside.

"What's your damage?" She tosses her purse onto the

table next to the door, then kicks off her shoes.

I barely hold my sigh in. She's standing in the middle of the entryway with me practically pressed up against the door, demanding answers like *I'm* the asshole in this situation.

"You're kidding, right?" Her pursed lips tell me she's not, and this time I do let my sigh out. "I don't have a key, River. Still. I've been staying here for a while now and I have no way to come and go as I please."

"I've been busy. I haven't had the chance to get to the store and get you your own copy."

"For two weeks?"

"For two weeks?" She mocks me like she's twelve. "Yes. In case you haven't realized, I run a business."

"Oh, trust me—the repeated interrupted nights of sleep make me aware of just how busy with work you are."

Though she promised to bring her laptop home from work, she keeps "forgetting." At this point, I'm certain she's getting off on making me miserable.

She doesn't look the least bit apologetic, and I know I'm not going to get anywhere with this.

"Can you please just get me a key? I truly don't think that's too much to ask."

"I—"

"If not for me," I cut her off, "then at least do it for Leo. He needs care and attention."

Her gaze drifts toward the terrarium set up on the console and the adorable creature lounging inside.

With a huff, she rolls her eyes back my way. "I'll make it a priority—I'll go first thing in the morning. Why are you coming and going on a Sunday anyway?"

"I was at the shelter earlier, then I met up with a friend. I do have a life, you know."

"You have friends?"

"Why is that surprising?"

"Because I can't imagine someone being friends with you willingly."

I push off the door, closing the distance between us. "I have plenty of friends, River."

"Sounds exactly like something a person with no friends would say. I wouldn't be surprised if you left the apartment every day to sit at the park by yourself just to make it look like your life isn't sad."

"That's real rich coming from you. You forget, we've been neighbors for a year now. I've seen you come home alone many nights over the months."

She tips her nose up. "I have standards."

"Or maybe it's because you can't get a guy to take you home."

She inhales a sharp breath, my words stinging. Her chest heaves, and she's close enough that I can feel her breasts ghost against my body. I'd be a fucking liar if I said my dick didn't jump at the almost contact.

Shit. Even when she's on my last damn nerve, like right now, I want to kiss her.

What the fuck is wrong with me?

It's all I've been able to think about.

It's on my mind first thing in the morning when she's in the kitchen making her coffee and whistling that same annoying tune she always does. When she glowers at me for waking up and existing. When she comes home from work looking stressed and tired. At night when I'm lying on that shitty air mattress praying for sleep.

I think about it all. The. Damn. Time.

It's slowly killing me. This whole week has been torture.

The worst part? It doesn't seem like it's affected River at all.

I need to know if it has.

Her lips curl back in a snarl. "Ass."

"Ouch. I'm *so* wounded by your super-smart insult."

"Dick."

"Yep, I have one, baby."

She glances pointedly at my crotch. "Could have fooled me."

I clench my teeth together. "That was cold, but I guess I shouldn't have expected anything less from the Ice Queen herself."

"I'm only cold toward you."

"Says the girl who obviously spends more time curled up on her couch alone rather than out with friends."

"Are you implying that *I* don't have any friends because I'm cold?"

"You implied I didn't first."

"Because I've met you!"

"And *I've* met *you*."

She sniffs haughtily, spinning away from me and putting distance between us.

I let out a quiet relieved breath, hoping she doesn't hear it.

"I have plenty of friends, thank you very much." She moves into the kitchen, reaching into the cabinet beside the fridge and pulling down a glass. "I just prefer to spend my nights by myself."

"You sure had that excuse locked and loaded, didn't you?

I'm just saying, you should get out more. Take up a hobby. Your social calendar is undoubtedly not full."

I've hit a nerve. I can see it in her jaw, the way it tics.

"I have hobbies."

"Like?"

"Avoiding you."

"Good luck with that since we're living together now."

"And at that reminder, I need a fucking drink." She groans, muttering something, but the only word I can make out clearly is *regret*.

She bends, getting into the cabinet under the toaster. A bottle of whiskey settles heavily on the counter, and she pops the top off, pouring two fingers' worth of booze into her glass.

Without hesitation, she tosses the alcohol back, then pours a refill.

"I—"

She holds her finger up, tosses back the second drink.

"Ah." She smacks her lips together. "Much better. Maybe now I can deal with you. Now, what did you want to insult me with next?"

"You're drinking your whiskey wrong. It's meant to be savored, not guzzled like a cheap shot."

With a roll of her eyes, she pours another drink...and slings it back.

Her gaze drops to the bottle and she shrugs. "You know what? Fuck it." She grabs the bottle and glass, padding down the hall. "I'm taking a bath. If I drown, I'm haunting your ass!"

The bathroom door slams closed, and I can't help but laugh.

Nolan was right.

River does challenge me like no one else ever has... especially my sanity.

Which is probably why I find myself stalking toward her like a maniac.

She doesn't react when I push the door open, almost like she was expecting me to follow her. Her whiskey is sitting on the counter, and she's bent over the tub in nothing but her t-shirt and underwear, messing with the water.

Her ass is in the air, and it brings back all the memories of her yoga session, which I've conjured up way too many times for it to be considered healthy.

Being close to her all the time...it's getting in my head. Making me notice things about her. Forcing me to see her when she's not so damn strung out all the time.

It's making me like her. Making me want to be around her, and not just to annoy her.

"Are those turtles on your ass?"

"Yes."

I narrow my eyes. "I thought you hated turtles."

"Why would you assume that?"

"Because you hate Leo and always make fun of him."

"Correction." She reaches over and turns the water back off. "I hate *you* and make fun of you. Now can you go? You're ruining my bath."

When she spins around, I waste no time crowding her against the sink, caging her in.

Her body presses tightly to mine, and everything inside my brain short-circuits when I feel her breasts.

She's soft and fits against me like that's where she's meant to be.

"W-What are you doing, Dean?" Her tongue peeks out,

tracing her plump lips that look so, *so* good.

I lean toward her, wanting to taste them. *Needing* to taste them.

"What am I doing?"

Shit. What *am* I doing?

Why do I have this ridiculous desire to touch her? To taste her?

It's River! This makes no sense.

And yet, here I am…staring down at her lips, which all too often spew words of hate.

But none of that matters in this moment.

I *need* to kiss her.

"I'm going to kiss you." Her breath hitches, and I look into her eyes. "Can I kiss you?"

Her head moves almost imperceptibly.

Then, I fucking *kiss* River White.

And she kisses me back.

Hard.

Her arms go around my neck, her fingers crashing through my already messy hair. I paw at her like a drug fiend who's afraid of never getting another hit, running my hands up and down her sides, over her ass. All over her. Too fucking scared I won't get to touch her again.

My cock grows impossibly hard, and there's no way she doesn't feel it pressing against her. I take a chance and rock into her. She gasps.

I do it again.

Another gasp.

Without warning, she yanks away, and we're both gasping for air like we just finished a marathon we were ill-prepared for.

"What... What the... I... We..."

Then our mouths are fused together again.

I don't know who reaches for who first. Don't know whose arms go around who first. Don't know how I'm ever going to pretend I don't know what her lips feel like.

I am so completely fucked.

I slow my mouth, turning our frenzied kiss into something calmer until our lips aren't moving at all. I close my eyes, resting my forehead against hers.

"I...fuck," I mutter.

She chuckles. "I agree."

Opening my eyes, I pull back, looking at her. "What was that?"

"I don't know. You're the one who accosted me."

"You're the one who didn't push me away."

"You're the one who liked it...though I guess I did too." She swallows. "Why?"

I grin. "Have you seen me shirtless?"

She doesn't laugh. Her hazel eyes just burn into me.

I can practically see her thoughts running through her head. They're the same ones charging through mine.

Why did I kiss her? What does it mean? What do we do now?

I don't know. I don't know. And I don't fucking know.

All I know is that I want to do it again.

"Why'd you do that, Dean?"

"Because I couldn't *not* do it."

"It can't mean anything. I hate you."

"I don't want it to mean anything because I hate you too."

Then, we're kissing again.

Chapter 13

RIVER

"YOU'RE EARLY! Did hell freeze over?!" Maya clutches her chest dramatically as I walk into Making Waves. She glides toward me, grabbing the tray of coffees from my hand. "Oh, wait—never mind. You're *always* early."

"Ha. Funny." If only I had something to throw at the smartass. "But I don't see how my punctuality is a bad thing."

"It's a bad thing when you virtually live at work." Caroline reaches over the counter, plucks a coffee from the tray, and takes a sip of the piping hot liquid, staring at me over the rim with accusing eyes.

"Oh, I'm sorry, did you *not* want help with inventory today?"

She grimaces, wiping the small trace of lip gloss from the lid of her cup. "I hate inventory."

"That's what I thought." I set the bag of turnovers I'm holding on the counter, grabbing my own coffee. "I brought breakfast."

"Bless you. I am *starving*. I left my protein bar at home by accident."

Maya, who doesn't typically eat sugar in the mornings, snatches the bag away, ripping it open and taking a huge bite from the first treat she can get her hands on. "Blech. Blueberry." She shoves it back inside and reaches for something else.

"Maya!"

"What? You know I hate blueberry." I can barely understand her as she talks with her mouth full, pulling another turnover from the bag. "Ha! I see the strawberry coming out of this. Dibs!"

She bites into it, moaning as she chews, and swallows the treat I wanted for myself.

Finding her manners again, she retrieves a napkin from the tray and wipes her mouth. "I know you're a complete workaholic, but why are you here half an hour early?"

"I was up early. Couldn't sleep."

Maya frowns, hopping up onto the counter, sitting cross-legged. She knows I hate it, but I don't say anything today. "Did you try your medication? I know you only like to take it for emergencies, but maybe this is one?"

"I'm not at that point yet."

"How much sleep did you get last night?"

"About three hours."

"Oh, you're right then. Definitely not at the point of medication. How could you be? I mean, you got *three whole hours* of sleep. No need for more." Caroline sips on her coffee like she's that damn Kermit meme and it's "none of her business."

I glare at her. "You are so not helpful today."

She laughs, not scared of me. "You know I'm just giving you crap—though I am worried." Her lips pull down at the corners. "Do you need a break from the store?"

"No way! No. It's nothing like that. My lack of sleep actually wasn't my insomnia at all."

Maya's eyes widen. "Did you and Dean bang?"

"What? No!"

My heart races at the suggestion because all I can think about is *the kiss*.

I'm not sure who stopped kissing who first, but Dean didn't say a word as he left the bathroom. He retreated to his room, and I climbed into the tub with my whiskey and didn't come out for nearly two hours. It was a miracle I wasn't hungover afterward.

I was too scared to come out and face him because kissing Dean Evans was the best kiss of my life.

I want to do it again. And again.

Immediately. Forever.

Her shoulders deflate. "Oh. Boo. What's going on then?"

Shit. Think of something, River. Think of something pronto!

"My back, from skating last week. I'm still sore."

She raises her brows. "Still?"

"Yes. I fell no less than ten times. Not like I'll heal overnight."

"Are you sure that's it?"

No. "Of course."

"I still can't believe you went out on a date with Dean."

I sigh at Caroline's statement. "It wasn't a date."

"Oh, it totally was. A lame date, too. You didn't even kiss." I whip my head toward Maya, snatching the breakfast *I* bought from her hands. "Hey! Give that back!" She scrambles for the turnover.

"No. Turnovers are for people who *aren't* assholes."

She pouts. "You're just annoyed I'm right."

I laugh derisively. "Please. You couldn't be more wrong."

"So you did kiss?"

"No!"

That's not a complete lie. We didn't kiss during roller skating.

We waited an entire week, an exceptionally long week where we pretended nothing happened. Dancing around each other in the apartment even more than we already had been. Bickering and arguing and picking at each other even more than usual.

Until finally, Dean made his move.

My lips are still tingling.

"You two should kiss. Or something. You've been crushing on him long enough."

"Caroline!"

Her baby blues widen as she feigns innocence though she's far from it. "What? I didn't realize it was a secret."

"Wait—she confessed she has a crush to you?" Maya asks Caroline. "I tried getting her to and she wouldn't budge."

"No confession, but I mean, come on"—Caroline gestures toward me—"it's obvious."

"I didn't confess because there is nothing to confess. I do *not* have a crush."

"Sure you don't." Maya shrugs. "Just like I don't have a crush on Henry Cavill and haven't masturbated to him at least three times this week."

Caroline gasps. "It's Wednesday, you horndog!"

Maya winks at her, and they both bust out into giggles.

"You two are starting to wear me out just as much as Dean

does." I take another big gulp of my coffee, needing it to deal with them.

"For someone who doesn't have a crush, you sure do talk about him a lot."

Maya looks damn proud of herself for saying that, until she sees the look on my face.

"He hasn't even been living there that long. What's he up to now?" she asks. "Oh, man. You haven't killed him already, have you? Is that what's stressing you out? Body disposal? You know I listen to those true crime podcasts—I can help with that."

"First of all, thank you. I'm happy to know if I were to ever pick up the pastime of murder, you'd have my back." She beams at me. "It's not one specific thing with Dean. It's *everything*. He's noisy. He eats my eggs *and* uses my creamer. He smells like"—*heaven*—"the gym. And his biggest flaw of all? He exists."

Caroline tucks her lips together, her eyes flitting to Maya, who is also fighting a smile. They're looking at each other like they share a secret, and I want in on it.

"What?"

They don't answer.

"Seriously? Why are you two smiling at each other like that?"

Maya hops off the counter. "Look, I'm only going to say this once, and I'm going to say it from a safe distance because you're tired and more likely to throw something at me." She blows out a dramatic breath. "You sound like one of those kids on the playground who pulls pigtails or says the kid they're crushing on is gross or has cooties. You might keep refuting it, but you need to take a good hard look at *why* you're pushing so hard for us to believe you. It's okay to like Dean, River."

"Ugh. I—"

I snap my mouth shut as she lifts her perfectly shaped brows.

"We're not going to judge you. In fact, it might be good for you. Maybe you can finally get laid." She wags her brows. "Or, you know, focus on something other than work."

I drag my gaze to Caroline, who's nodding and staring at me just like Maya is.

They think I have a crush. Think I'm just burying it. Denying it.

They're wrong.

I *don't* like Dean.

His damn music and guitar playing keeps me up. He steals my pie. He has an emotional support turtle, for Pete's sake.

Sure, he's smart and can be funny when he's not busy driving me insane. And, yeah, he has a stable career, and let's not forget how undeniably attractive he is…or that these are all things I'm looking for in a relationship.

But he's *Dean*.

We have nothing in common other than our love of pie.

We'd never work.

Plus, I hate him.

I *can't* like him…right?

It doesn't matter that I like the way his eyes caress me. Doesn't matter that when he touches me, even just a whisper of contact, I feel it everywhere.

And it really doesn't matter that when he kissed me, it felt like everything I've been missing was suddenly found.

He's *Dean*. I can't be putting silly thoughts like that in my head about my new roommate, especially when it's him.

Pushing my chest out, I raise my chin.

"You're wrong. I do not have a crush."

The words sound weak even to my own ears.

Oh hell.

They could have a point after all.

I have a crush on Dean.

I'M NOT good at not working. It's just not in my blood.

But tonight, I didn't bat a lash when the clock struck seven and I clicked the sign to *Closed*.

For the first time in I don't even know how long, I'm riding the elevator up to my floor at seven thirty.

I don't want to be at work. I want to be at home.

I'm trying not to analyze what that could possibly mean as I step out of the car.

I pause when I see Dean standing in the hallway.

The last time he was standing out here, it ended in a kiss.

Is it wrong to hope that will happen again?

We haven't talked about the kiss from three nights ago. We're not actively avoiding one another, but neither of us has made a move to talk…or kiss again. We're just co-existing. It feels like some sort of barrier has been broken down, but we're both too afraid to truly cross it.

Slowly, I make my way toward him.

He's leaning against the wall opposite his apartment, arms crossed over his chest, not paying any attention to me.

He's ditched his tie for summer school, but I'm surprised

to see he's still wearing his work attire since I finally had a key made for him yesterday. Surely he hasn't lost it already.

Then again, if he had it, I'd miss this view.

He looks good…too damn good.

The evening sunlight is filtering in at the end of the hall, and it's casting a soft glow that makes it look like he's in one of those cologne commercials that are overly sexual and make zero sense.

Gorgeous. Poster-worthy.

I take another step toward him—then freeze when I hear it.

A giggle.

It's coming from inside his apartment.

A girl with dark hair bends under the caution tape that's been put up.

Dean smiles at her. "Enjoy yourself?"

"Immensely."

He shakes his head. "You're never going to stop teasing me, are you?"

"Not a chance."

"Shit."

She laughs again, shoving at him playfully. She looks vaguely familiar, and I think it's one of the girls Dean's had over in the past.

She's gorgeous. Absolutely stunning. Tall and slender. She looks like she could be in one of those perfume commercials too.

I'm reminded why something between Dean and me could never work—he's a grade-A dick.

He's either screwing around behind this chick's back, or he's leading me on.

I won't stand for either.

"Come on," she says. "Let's go grab something to eat. Then we can go for round two."

They turn toward me, and I duck behind the nearest thing I can find—the potted plant I apologize to almost weekly because I'm always running into it.

"River?"

Shit. Busted.

I peek out from around the fern. "Oh. Hi. Didn't see you there."

Dean's eyes are wide. He's surprised to see me. "You're home early."

Yep. Sorry to ruin your date with my presence. I'm just the girl you kissed senseless the other night. No big deal.

I clear my throat. "Yep." *I'm here to see you.* "Just got done with work early for a change."

My eyes flit to the pretty girl, and I give her the brightest smile I can scrounge up.

She returns it, looking between me and Dean with curious eyes.

"I, uh, I've been meaning to introduce you to someone. This is—"

"Actually, I have to be...Morris. I need to take care of Morris."

Dean's brows scrunch together. "He's fine. I just checked on him."

"It's a cat mom thing. You wouldn't get it." I brush past him and his date. I slip my key into the doorknob and twist, then turn back to the duo. "Don't worry—I won't wait up."

I race inside my apartment as fast as I can, slamming the door closed and collapsing back on it.

What in the hell? Who does he think he is? Why would he be so nonchalant about it? Why wouldn't he tell me he was seeing someone before *he kissed me?*

My mind is spinning, and I take in a few deep breaths, trying to calm myself, but it's hard.

I'm fuming. So damn angry I'm vibrating.

Wait…no.

That's the door.

Dean shoves into the apartment, moving me like I weigh nothing, and to him I probably do.

The door slams back closed with my weight on it, and all I can think is this must be awkward for his lady friend out in the hall.

He towers over me, hands on his hips, his usually bright green eyes at least two shades darker.

"What the hell was that?" His voice is low, near a whisper.

"What was what?"

"River…"

"Dean…" I mock his deep tone.

Then his big arms are boxing me in, my back ramrod straight against the door. He's close. So close I can almost *taste* the cinnamon on his breath.

"Just talk to me, River. Don't skirt around what's bothering you."

I meet his strong stare. "I'm not happy with you."

"That much I gathered. Want to tell me why?"

"You kissed me. You kissed me and now today you're with some other girl. You tell me to talk to you, but you failed to talk to me when you didn't mention to me that you're seeing someone."

"I fucking swear…" he mutters, closing his eyes. When he

peels them open, they're darker. "If you would have taken *two seconds* to meet her, you'd know the girl standing out in the hallway isn't someone I'm seeing and hiding from you. She's my little sister."

His…sister?

Oh no. I *do* remember him mentioning having a sister before, but I didn't pay much attention to any details about her other than that she still lives in their hometown.

"I…oh."

Shit. I just acted like a jealous moron over his sister. *His sister!*

What the hell did that kiss do to me?

"Yeah. *Oh.*"

"I…didn't know."

"I got that. I'm just trying really hard not to be offended by the fact that you think I walk around kissing people when I'm in an alleged relationship."

"I didn't know," I say again, this time quieter.

"That's not who I am." He slides closer, fitting himself against me. I can feel him growing hard, and that ache that's been building inside of me since he moved in has me on edge. "I kiss with a purpose."

"Then why haven't you kissed me again?"

"Because you haven't asked."

My chest is heaving. I'm begging for air and begging for him to get closer all at once.

I *need* Dean to kiss me again.

"Dean?"

He drives his hips forward, and I gasp.

"Yeah?"

"Kiss me again."

He laughs, and it's dark, his devilish side coming out to play. "No."

I groan, bouncing my head off the door twice. "Why not?"

He dips his head, his lips trailing over the soft skin of my neck. Up, up, up until they're at my ear.

I want to lean into the tantalizing touch, but I resist.

I've embarrassed myself enough tonight.

"If I kiss you again, River," he whispers, those damn lips brushing against me with every syllable, "I won't stop."

"Is that such a bad thing?"

"It is when I want to make you wait. And when I have plans." He pulls away from me, his eyes pained at the thought of walking away without a kiss.

"Right. Your sister. That girl in the hallway."

My cheeks redden, and it's not only because Dean just had me pressed against the door with his obviously hard cock rubbing up on me.

He chuckles at my embarrassment. "If it makes you feel any better, she's aware you thought we were dating and not only will she make fun of me for it, she'll hit me with about ten thousand questions on why you'd react the way you did."

"And what will you tell her?"

"That you kissed me, and now you want to kiss me again and turn it into a whole thing like sex and whatnot." He waves his hand about.

"I never said *anything* about sex! And *you* kissed *me*!"

"I plead temporary insanity."

"And this?" I point between us. "Just now?"

"You're a witch. You used magic on me. A seduction spell."

"They'll stone me to death."

"Then it was nice knowing you."

I snort. "Glad to know you still hate me."

"Do you?"

"Do I what?"

"Do you still hate me?"

I...don't know.

The Dean who's my roommate seems different than the Dean who steals my pie. Different than the one who blasts loud, awful music. He even infuriates me on a different level now—sexually.

He's still plenty obnoxious in his own right, but I'm beginning to believe I might have misjudged him before.

And it's not just because his kisses make me feel like I'm on fire in all the best ways.

It's deeper than that.

"I'm not sure. Do you still hate me?"

One side of his lips curves up, and he looks to the floor, rubbing at the back of his head. "I don't think I ever did."

My heart flutters.

Wait—nope.

That's the damn door again.

"Dude! Deanie Weenie! Did you get lost in there?" His sister bangs on the door. "Are we still doing dinner? I'm starving and have been craving The Gravy Train."

"Deanie Weenie?" I lift a brow his way.

Face pale, he gulps. "Pretend you didn't hear that."

"Oh, no. I want details."

I turn on my heel and pull open the front door. His sister stumbles back slightly but quickly composes herself.

She grins at me, her big white smile almost blinding. "You must be the neighbor I've heard so much about."

"Huh." I peek over at Dean. "Have you been talking about me, *Deanie Weenie?*"

The death stare he gives his sister *almost* makes *me* break out in hives. He looms over both of us, hands on his hips, stance menacing.

His anger simmers in his eyes. "I'm going to murder you."

She waves his threat off. "Please. Then who will deal with your father for you?" She turns to me. "I'm Holland."

"River."

"I'm sure you're wondering where Dean got his nickname."

I bob my head. "Very much so."

"Holland, don't you dare."

I turn to him, patting his chest. "Hush."

"When he was a kid, he *loved* to be naked. He'd strip down to nothing whenever and wherever he could, then start flapping his *weenie* in the wind like that helicopter move." She wiggles her hips like I've seen guys do before. "He'd shout, *Deanie's Weenie, Deanie's Weenie!*" She shrugs. "Naturally, it stuck…and so did the nightmares."

Dean swears and pinches the bridge of his nose. "I regret inviting you to dinner."

"Good thing you didn't invite me."

"That's right—you just texted me and showed up."

"I wanted to see the damage you did to your apartment in person." She shakes her head and grins my way. "Can you believe this idiot? Threw water on a grease fire."

"Oh, I can believe it—I witnessed it."

"I'm so sorry. I thought our parents raised him better than that. Paid for that fancy private school and college and everything. Still so dense."

"Okay," Dean says, playfully shoving his sister toward the door. "You're done. Out you go. We're leaving."

"Aw, so soon?" She shoots me another smile, fighting against him. "It was great to finally meet you. I love the items you sell at your shop. We'll have to chat longer next time."

She knows about my shop?

"This will be the only time you two ever meet if I have anything to say about it."

Dean pushes her out the door, closing it in her face as she laughs.

He holds the door closed with one arm and peers down at me.

"Ignore everything she just said. She's not well."

"I think she's perfectly fine."

"You're just confused right now."

"You're right. I did just ask you of all people to kiss me...*again*. Clearly, my judgment cannot be trusted."

"I take mild offense to that." He clears his throat, eyes growing serious. "We, uh, we should probably talk about... whatever is happening, huh?"

He looks as nervous as I feel because what in the hell is happening? What are we doing?

"That might be a good idea."

"When I get back from dinner? Wait up for me?"

I nod.

He shoots me that smirk that's starting to grow on me, then walks out the door, not taking his eyes off me the whole time.

And my heart flutters again.

Chapter 14

DEAN

"YOU TWO KISSED."

I glare at my annoying little sister. "Shut up, Holland."

"Is that a confirmation?"

"That's a shut up and mind your own business."

"That's totally a yes."

We make our way down the hall to the elevator and press the button for the car.

"You know, I always thought you might have a thing for her." She bumps her shoulder into mine.

I grunt, and she laughs.

"It's not what you think," I say.

"So something *is* going on between you two?"

Is there? We kissed and it felt amazing, but I'm not entirely sure what it means…or if it means anything at all.

It'd be absurd to think there could be something between us…wouldn't it?

It's River we're talking about. We've been enemies since the moment I moved my first box into my apartment and Morris got out, snuck into my place, and clawed up my couch. There hasn't been a moment after when she hasn't hated me.

How could something between us actually work?

"I'm not sure," I tell Holland.

"Do you want there to be?"

"I'm...not sure." She nods like she understands, though there's no way she does because *I* don't understand. "I think I like her, but we've not always been on the best of terms."

"I hear hate sex is good."

I glance down at her. "I thought we agreed we'd never discuss our sex lives."

"I said I *heard*, not that I was speaking from experience. But now that you mention it..."

I shake my head, covering my ears. "No. Nope. Don't even think about it."

She rolls her eyes. "But you did kiss her though, right?"

Irritated, I toss my head back. "Yes, we kissed."

"Ha! I knew it!"

"It was just once."

Lie.

It was more than once. Hell, it was a full-blown make-out session.

It was more than a kiss, but it hasn't happened since then.

Not for lack of wanting, but because I don't know how she'd react if I gave in to the urges I have when it comes to her. I don't know what River wants out of this. I don't know what *I* want out of this.

I just know I want to touch her again.

I want to taste her again.

And soon.

"Ew. You're totally thinking about kissing her right now, aren't you?"

Yes. "No."

"Liar."

"Shut up, Holland."

She laughs, and I know it's going to be a long night.

MY JAW DROPS when I push open the door to River's apartment.

Ass.

That's exactly what's on display. River's bent and twisted in some pose I couldn't tell you the name of if my life depended on it.

She's wearing nothing but a camisole top and a pair of that underwear that looks like boxer briefs for ladies.

A man could get used to coming home to a sight like this.

"You're home," she says as she maneuvers herself into an upright position. "I thought you'd be out much later."

"I thought so too. My sister talks a lot," I tell her, closing the front door and toeing off my shoes. Morris runs over and starts to sniff at them. He'll likely run off with one of them before the night is over just to spite me. "Duty called though. Holland had to bail early."

And by duty, I mean our father and some asinine request that could have waited until morning.

But I don't want to think about my asshole father.

I want to focus on what's right in front of me.

River.

More specifically, River in her panties, ass in the air.

"Doing some yoga?"

She nods. "Had some…tension to work through."

"I see." I saunter into the apartment, taking a seat at one of the stools at the kitchen island. "Well, don't let me stop you. Please, continue." I don't even bother hiding my smirk.

Neither does River.

No, she bends again, sticking her ass out just for me.

I physically bite my knuckles to keep from reaching out to her.

And I want to reach out. *Bad.*

I want to run my fingers over her curves. Want to feel the weight of her under my hands. I want to see if she's as flexible in bed as I'm guessing she is.

My cock gets hard just thinking about it.

I spread my legs, adjusting myself.

"Perv," she says.

"Tease," I counter.

She's not wrong. I am being a perv right now—but I don't see her running away or making any attempts to hide herself.

No, she's not doing any of that.

River likes my eyes on her just as much as I like watching.

She finishes her session, and I don't dare move from the stool the entire time, though it's hard to hold back.

When she's done, she pads into the kitchen for a glass of water.

I watch the entire time she does that too.

"How was your dinner?" she asks, eyeing me over the rim of her glass.

"Is that really what you want to talk about right now?"

"No." With a sigh, she sets the glass in the sink and rests her hands on the counter behind her. "Why'd you kiss me, Dean?"

"I already told you why."

"Not really. You said you did it because you couldn't *not* kiss me. That's not a real answer."

"Isn't it?"

"No. It's a cop-out. You almost kissed me at the roller rink too, didn't you?"

I nod. "If Lucy hadn't interrupted us, I would have."

"Why?"

I push off of my stool and stalk around the island until I'm standing opposite her, mirroring her position. "For the same reason as when I finally did kiss you."

"Wh—"

I shake my head, and her mouth stops moving.

"Stop asking why, River. I don't know why. I'm not one to dance around crap. If I had an answer beyond what I already gave you, I'd tell you. Can't we just let this happen how it's happening and stop questioning it?"

"Can we? Because I don't know about you, but it freaks me out. Does it not weird you out that suddenly we want to jump each other's bones when we've been at each other's throats for the last year?"

"It definitely interests me that you want to jump my bones."

"Dean…" she grumbles.

I laugh. "I'm kidding. Kind of. But, also, is it really all that surprising? I mean, we're living together now. We're seeing more of each other, in close quarters and with close contact. Last I checked, we're two single adults who have been single for quite some time. We're under stress and likely undersexed. It wouldn't be completely insane for us to take advantage of the situation we're in and relieve some of that tension."

She chews on her bottom lip, mulling my words over as she stares at the floor in the space between us.

I don't believe what I'm saying is far from the truth. It's what I came up with during dinner with Holland. She was yammering on about something to do with work, and I didn't have any interest in paying attention.

My thoughts drifted to River almost immediately.

I'm not wrong. We *are* spending more time together, seeing each other in a whole new light. There's bound to be a discovery of new desirability.

Besides, if we're truly being honest with ourselves, there's always been some level of attraction between us.

What's that saying? Love and hate are two sides of the same coin?

If there's one thing that's become clear to me since living with River, it's that I don't hate her.

Not at all.

"Do you think I'm wrong?" I ask her.

"No. That seems like a fair assessment of our situation."

"I agree."

"And you kissing me is, what? Relieving tension? Is that what you want to do? Be make-out buddies?"

I laugh.

Kiss her?

Oh, kissing is just the beginning of what I want to do to her.

I want to see what makes her scream. What makes her toes curl. What causes her to beg and plead. I want to see her climb to the highest peaks and fall back down over and over again. Want to see how she looks at her most vulnerable.

I want to do a whole lot more than just relieve tension with a quickie.

"I want to fuck you, River." Her throat bobs at my candidness, and I take a step forward. "It won't just be a one-off thing, because I'm kind of greedy like that." Another step. "I want to take my time. Learn your body. Your quirks. Your weaknesses. I want to learn *you*."

Her breaths are coming in sharper, chest heaving with...*anticipation*?

She likes the sound of this as much as I do.

"Are you proposing friends with benefits?"

I pull my lips up. "Did you just call us friends?" Reaching out, I brush my fingers along the skin that's peeking out between her shirt and underwear. Her skin pebbles at the light touch. "Told you you're getting a soft spot for me."

"And I thought we agreed you've gone temporarily insane."

I must have, haven't I? Here I am suggesting to the girl who hates me that we start some sort of sexual arrangement while she's allowing me to live in her apartment.

She laughs, probably thinking the same thing.

"No labels then," she says. "No pressure. It just is what it is."

"Just a thing we're doing, not making a big deal out of it."

"Right. And no butt stuff. No sleeping around with other people either."

"We can circle back around to that butt-stuff conversation later." She grins, shaking her head. "And when my apartment is ready...?"

"This is done. No attachments. We go back to being

neighbors. No making it awkward. We're just relieving tension is all."

I nod. "Agreed. So, is this your way of saying you want to do this? I need a clear answer on this one, River."

She blows out a deep breath, then closes the distance between us. I wrap my arm around her waist, and she sighs when I pull her close, like she's been waiting all night to feel me again.

"I'm either completely desperate or just as insane as you..." She tilts her head back, looking up at me. "Yes, I—"

I kiss her.

She moans and kisses me back with just as much force.

Is it crazy to say I've missed this? Missed her mouth on mine. Missed the way her body feels under my hands. The sounds she makes. Her eagerness.

Her.

Yeah, buddy, that's pretty damn crazy.

Ah, fuck it. I like a little crazy.

I sweep my hands down her curves, slide them under her ass, and pull her up, spinning her to set her on top of the island.

"What are you doing?" she asks, breaking the connection between our mouths.

"Trying to kiss you. Stop talking."

"No." She pushes on me and I step back, heeding her request and giving her space. She laughs, then grabs my shirt, pulling me back to her. "Not *no*. Just *not in here* no."

"What? Why not? Do you know how many times I've thought about you laid out on this very counter?"

Her hazel eyes surge with craving. "Because I'm pretty sure I can feel Leo staring at us and it's weird."

I glance at him over her shoulder, and she's right. He *is* staring at us.

"You trying to cockblock me, little man? I thought we were tighter than that."

River giggles, and I realize then that I could listen to that sound for the rest of my days and not get tired of it.

"Take me to your bedroom."

"My bedroom? You want to fuck on an air mattress?"

She scrunches her face up. "Good point. Let's go to my room."

She doesn't have to tell me twice.

I swoop her into my arms, and she locks her legs around my waist as I take long strides down the hallway, not wasting any time.

She lets out little sounds every time my dick brushes against her, and I can't fucking wait to hear what she sounds like when I'm inside her.

"Might want to close the door," she says when I reach her room.

I lift a brow in question but follow her instruction.

"Morris," she explains. "He'll probably try to attack you if he sees you on top of me."

"Oh, you just assume *I'm* going to be on top, huh?" I drop her onto the edge of the bed unceremoniously. Towering over her, I stare down as she blinks up at me with amused eyes. "If you think I'm doing all the work, you're nuts."

With a roll of her eyes, she hooks a finger into the belt loop on my pants and drags me closer, pushes the belt through the buckle. As she works to undo it, I quickly undo the buttons of my dress shirt. I'm flinging the material across the room when her fingers find my zipper, and the sound is loud as she drags it down the track.

She works my pants down my thighs, and if possible, I swear I get harder when she rolls her tongue over her lips as she sees my dick straining against my boxer briefs.

"What are you doing, River?" My voice is rough and scratchy, and I have to work to get the words out.

"Sucking your cock."

"I was kidding."

She peeks up at me with heavy eyes. "I'm not."

Her fingernails scrape lightly over my thighs as she drags my briefs down and frees my erection.

She wastes no time before touching me, wrapping her hand around my dick and giving me a light stroke.

I can definitely tell it's been too long because that one touch feels way too good.

She leans closer and brings her mouth to me, flattening her tongue and stroking it along the underside of my cock.

I might die.

"Fucking hell," I mutter.

Her eyes flit to mine. "Will you hold my hair?"

I almost come just from her request alone.

I slide my hand into her hair, wrapping the long red locks around my fist and pulling them up.

"Tighter," she tells me, and my dick jumps.

Fuck. "Are you trying to embarrass me and make me come way too fucking soon?"

She doesn't answer.

She can't.

Her lips are too busy being fitted around my straining cock.

"Son of a…" I grip her hair tighter.

With a torturous pace, she slides her mouth over me, and I watch as I disappear inch by inch.

She holds my stare as she begins to work me over with just her mouth, sucking and using her tongue to torture me as I help guide her in a rhythm that I love. With every stroke, she takes me deeper, and with every stroke, I get closer and closer to the edge.

She scrapes her fingernails along my thighs, and the bite of pain makes me curse in the best way.

She giggles and does it again.

I had it right before—River is *definitely* a witch.

When she tries to drag her mouth off me, I tighten my grip, and her eyes widen with excitement. I slowly drive her back down my length until I'm completely seated inside her mouth. She moans around me as I hold her there for a few beats, and I know if I keep this up, I will without a doubt blow my load straight down her throat.

It's too soon for that.

I rock my hips a few times, then loosen my grip. She eases up, popping off me with labored breaths.

"You good?"

She nods, eyes glassy with desire. "Do it again."

I laugh and shake my head. "Not this time."

"Dean…"

I release the red locks from my grasp and reach for her, pulling her onto her feet.

She's not wearing much, but I want her to be wearing less.

I grab the hem of her shirt and she raises her arms, helping me work it off her. I let it fall to the floor.

I peel the rest of my clothes off, then stand back to look at her. There's a soft glow from the moonlight coming in through the window across the room, and it hits her at all the right angles.

River's always beautiful.

But River standing topless in nothing but a pair of panties, her deep red mane a mess from my hands, a flush on her skin and a look in her eyes that says *Fuck me, please*?

It's a whole new look for her.

"You're gorgeous."

Her flush deepens.

I step into her, cupping her tits with my hands, running my thumbs over the hardened buds. I trail one hand down her stomach and straight into her panties.

I don't stop until my fingers find their way between her folds, and *my god* is she wet.

"Did my cock in your throat do this?"

A whimper.

A nod.

"Good."

I slip my fingers into her, and her breath hitches as she drops her head to my shoulder.

"Oh hell. I knew you were the devil."

I laugh and thrust my fingers deeper. I use my thumb to stroke her clit as I slide my other hand around the back of her neck and bring her lips to mine.

I kiss her, using my tongue in sync with the strokes of my fingers. She rocks into my hand, moaning and pulling at me, wanting more.

She wrenches her lips from mine. "Dean."

It's all she says, and I know she's ready.

I pull my hand from her body. "Get on the bed."

"What position?"

"Yes."

She laughs. "I'm serious."

"So am I," I say, grabbing her waist and guiding her backward. "I want you in all of them."

Her eyes darken as we fall onto the bed, and I drop my mouth to hers.

Without warning, I flip her over, putting her ass in the air just where I like it.

"Do you have any idea how long I've wanted to put you in this exact position?" I say, running my hands over her, squeezing. "Always teasing me with that yoga shit."

I give her a light smack, testing.

She moans.

I do it again.

"Talk about teasing," she says, pushing her ass out farther. "Just fuck me already."

"I want to taste you."

"Later. *Please.*"

I give her another smack. "Protection?"

"Nightstand. Top drawer."

"Don't move."

I roll off the bed to grab the condom. As I'm sliding it on, she begins to push her panties down, and I brush her hand away.

"No." I climb back into my position. "Mine."

"Ugh." She groans, wiggling her hips. "Would you hurry up at least?"

My lips at her ear, I say, "Do you really want to be bossing me around right now? Because I could drag this out all night."

"Do you really want to try to threaten *me* right now?

Because I could walk away from this and take care of myself with one of my many vibrators. Your call."

I swat her ass again and peel her panties off.

"That's what I thought," she says smugly. "Now, fuck me already."

I give my cock a couple tugs, then line myself up with her core, pushing into her heat.

"Oh shit..." I hiss as she begins to grip me. It has been *way* too long since I've felt anything this good. "Fuck."

"That's what I'm trying to do."

Thwack!

She whimpers at the smack to her ass, and I slide in slowly, watching as she stretches around my dick like it was made for her.

Gripping her hip with one hand, I move the other up her body to twist that hair of hers I'm really starting to love around my fist, and I hit home.

I swear I see stars.

She feels so fucking good. Better than I imagined. I know I'm going to have a hard time following the rules of *no getting attached* because I could *definitely* get attached to this feeling.

She cries out, and I slam into her again.

We find a rhythm as I drive into her, our skin smacking together, our breaths growing heavier and heavier. It doesn't take long until we're both teetering close to release.

"River?"

I slow my pace and lean down, capturing her mouth with mine, making short, quick thrusts.

"I'm close," she murmurs, answering my unvoiced question through the kisses.

"Thank fuck." I rest my forehead against her temple, pushing into her again. "Touch yourself. Get there with me."

She reaches a hand between her legs and plays with her clit, and I love that she's not afraid to do it.

"So close," she whispers. "More."

I thrust into her without restraint, and she cries out as her orgasm takes over, her pussy clenching around me, begging me to follow her over the edge.

I quicken my pace, and it's less than a minute before I'm following her to bliss.

She collapses onto the mattress, and I fall on top of her, dropping my head between her shoulders.

Our breaths are loud and harsh. We gasp for air, for any sort of reprieve.

"Well, that happened." She breaks the silence first.

I laugh, rolling off her and flopping onto my back, one arm under my head as I work to settle my breathing. "Yeah, it did."

We go silent, and the reality of what just transpired starts to set in.

As does the panic.

What in the hell are we thinking?! We can't do this! You don't just go back to normal after striking up a casual sex-only relationship with your neighbor/temporary roommate.

You're a dumbass, Dean. Complete and utter fucking moron. There's no way this is going to end well.

She rolls to her side, facing me.

"Hey, Dean?"

"Hmm?" I say, turning my head toward her.

"Want to go get some pie?"

And just like that, I know we're going to be okay.

Chapter 15

RIVER

A SOFT MELODY pulls me from my peaceful slumber.

The song is familiar, and it reverberates around my head like it's coming from somewhere close.

Like "*right* next to me" kind of close.

Though I'm not ready to wake up yet, I drag my eyes open and peer around.

Green. So much green.

Like my favorite chocolate candies. It makes me want M&M'S bad.

My stomach growls at the thought of food.

The bed shakes with laughter, and the music stops.

"Someone's hungry," Dean says, peering down at me, his guitar in his hands.

"If *someone* hadn't kept me up all night and had fed me properly, my stomach wouldn't be growling."

"Hey, you're the one who insisted on *only pie* and then another round."

"And you're the one who woke me up in the middle of the night for the next."

He doesn't look the least bit sorry, and honestly, for once I'm not the least bit upset by my lack of sleep. Even though

I'm sore in all the best ways possible, I feel like a million bucks. Worn out yet satiated…and maybe a little hungry for more.

He lifts a shoulder, grinning down at me. "Told you I was sex-deprived. Just trying to make up for all the months I went without."

"Right." I pull myself up to a sitting position, resting my back against the headboard. "I'm sure."

My shuffling around pulls at the blanket, and it falls dangerously low, drawing my eyes to his *very* obvious erection.

Unlike me, who threw my panties and camisole back on after my shower, Dean slept naked last night. I learned he's only been sleeping in boxer briefs because of me.

"Why does it sound like you don't believe me that it's been months since I've slept with someone?"

"Did you forget we're neighbors?"

"No?"

"I've seen the girls come in and out of your apartment over the last year. I'm aware you're not hurting for entertainment."

His black brows lift. "Been spying on me, River?"

"Please. I have so many better things to do with my time."

"Uh-huh. Like stay at home on your couch with your cookies and ice cream?"

"Oh my gosh. You saw me with a bag of snacks in the elevator *one time*."

"One time *a week*."

I flip him off. He laughs.

Then reaches to the nightstand, grabbing his cell phone and plunking it into my lap. "Call your optometrist."

"What?"

He nods toward the phone, moving his fingers back to the guitar strings, plucking at them mindlessly. "Your eye doctor—give them a call."

"Why?"

"Because clearly, you need your eyes checked."

I roll said eyes, tossing his phone back onto the bedside table. "Please. Do not try to sit here and tell me I'm seeing things."

"Oh, I'm not telling you you're seeing things. Just saying you're not paying attention to what's right in front of you. 'All those girls' you've been seeing? It's the same girl."

I crinkle my nose, shaking my head. "No, it's not."

"I can assure you, it is."

My eyes widen. "You're going to tell me that's your sister again, aren't you?"

His lips curve into a smile. "She colors her hair often—the one rebellious streak she has. I'm flattered you think I'm such a catch that I can score all the ladies all the time." He pats his bare chest. "Gives me the warm and fuzzies."

"Ugh." I swat at him, but he hides behind his guitar. "Shut up. I'm going back to bed. I already can't deal with you today."

I shimmy down the mattress, grabbing the blankets and pulling them up to my chin.

He laughs, and his fingers brush against the guitar strings.

That soft melody from before fills the room, and my eyes grow heavy quickly. It's so soothing, I might actually fall back asleep.

Then, I hear it.

It's soft. Quiet.

Beautiful.

I've complained about Dean's impromptu concerts on his balcony before, but truthfully, I love them.

I don't know how many nights I've sat in my living room with the windows open, listening to him play.

He doesn't sing often, but when he does, I stop whatever I'm doing and listen.

His voice isn't perfect. It's not like he has a crazy, untapped talent he's been hiding and will one day become some mega-superstar.

But it's good enough that it draws you in, makes you pay attention.

The chords fade and so does his voice, and I roll back over, peeking up at him.

"What song was that?"

"*Night Moves* by Bob Seger. One of my favorites. It's about fucking."

He winks at me, and I blush.

He continues to pluck the strings, and an ache begins to form between my thighs as I remember how his fingers felt on me…in me…last night.

I've never had sex three times in one night. Hell, I can't remember a time I had it more than once before. Other guys I've been with have always been a one-and-done kind of thing, and most of the time they didn't even care if I got off.

Not Dean.

He was attentive. *Very* attentive.

I felt adored. Sexy. In capable hands. He made me feel like he'd never get enough of me.

I already know if I'm not careful, I could get used to feeling like that.

When I push back up to a sitting position, he turns to me.

"Can I ask you something?" he says.

"In a minute."

I grab his guitar from his hands and set it on the floor next to the bed. I replace it with me.

I slip onto his lap and his hands automatically find my hips, fitting me against him like I belong there.

"What are you doing?"

"Kissing you."

I drop my lips to his and do just that.

He kisses me back, quickly taking control of the situation and sweeping his tongue along my lips. I open for him, letting him explore my mouth as I rock my hips against him, trying to find the friction I'm craving so much.

He chuckles, pulling away and smirking up at me. "Got a taste and now you can't get enough of me, huh?"

Moment ruined.

I roll my eyes and try to wiggle away, but he holds me in place.

"I'm teasing, I'm teasing. Don't go. I like the feeling of you up here. You feel good."

"Well, you ruined it, so"—I throw my hands in the air, then cross them over my chest—"might as well ask me what you were going to ask me."

He nods toward the other side of the room. "What's with the hole in the wall?"

I feel the color drain from my face.

Shit. My clit vibrator hole.

"Uh…"

Think of something. Think of something!

"The apartment came like that."

He tucks his lips together, trying not to laugh at that. "It came with a hole in the wall, huh?"

"Yep. It's decorative. Yours didn't come with that?"

Why the hell are you doubling down on this?!

"That's what you're going with?"

"Going with?" I push my chest out. "It's the truth."

"Uh-huh. It has nothing to do with the night you were in here masturbating and chucked something at the door when I scared you."

My mouth drops open.

He chuckles and reaches out with two fingers, pushing it closed.

"How did you know that?!"

Another laugh. "Well, I wasn't sure, but I am now."

I glower at him. "*This* is why I hate you."

"No it's not."

"How did you come to the conclusion that I was masturbating?"

"You definitely said my name when I walked by your room. You slung something at the door, and it was obvious you were startled, which means you were doing something *naughty*. I just put two and two together and assumed you were in there flicking your bean and thinking about me."

"Okay, first, absolutely *nobody* calls it that. It is not called a bean, and you certainly do not flick it. Do not *ever* flick my clit." I jam my finger into his chest with every word. "And second, do you really think I was masturbating to you and said your name when I came?"

"Absolutely."

He says it so confidently. He's so damn sure.

It's annoying how cocky he is.

And so fucking hot.

Ugh!

"You are absolutely delusional, you know that?"

"Tell me the flaw in my logic."

"I did not say your name at completion!"

"But you were masturbating?" He smirks like he just won a fucking prize.

I groan, tossing my head back.

The movement has my hips shifting and Dean grunting at the contact with his dick.

I do it again. Another grunt.

And again.

He jerks me to him, crashing his hands into my hair and pulling my lips back to his in a rough kiss. I don't stop moving my hips, and he doesn't stop kissing me until we're panting and needing more.

He wrenches his mouth away. "Do you still have it?"

I have no idea what he's talking about, and honestly, I don't even want to hear him talk right now. I just want to keep kissing him. I try to pull him back to me, but he resists.

I growl, frustrated. "Do I still have what?"

"Whatever you threw at the wall—your vibrator or dildo or whatever it was."

This time it's me who pulls back.

He's staring up at me, his eyes dark with need. "Do you?"

"Yes."

"Go get it."

His face is hard. Serious.

Holy crap. He means that.

I lean to the side, and he holds on to me as I reach into the bottom drawer of my bedside table and pull my toy free.

"That…does not look like I thought it would."

"What? You thought I was just in here riding on a big dong, pretending it was yours?"

"If that were the case, you would have been sorely disappointed when you saw the real thing and realized what you'd been missing out on this whole time."

I shake my head. "So sure of yourself."

Though he's not wrong…

He looks down at the toy, a bit of a mystified look on his face. "How do you use it?"

"It's a clit vibrator. You just…well, you put it on your clit and let it do its thing."

"Do it."

I pinch my brows together. "Huh?"

"Do it. Use it. I want to watch."

"Are you serious?"

"Yes. I told you I want to learn you. Should I not be serious?"

"I mean…" I chew on my lip, then shrug. "It's just that in my experience, guys aren't very receptive to toys in the bedroom. Makes them feel inadequate."

"Morons," Dean says. "That's such a bullshit way of saying it makes them jealous or that they don't want to learn. They should want their partner happy, and if it takes a toy, it takes a toy. Not saying they shouldn't also work at it but, I mean, fuck. It's sex, not rocket science."

I laugh.

I love how adamant he is about this, how he's not intimidated and just wants to make me happy.

Love it so much I can't help but press my lips to his.

He kisses me back hungrily, devouring my mouth like it's the last time we'll ever kiss.

His grip tightens, hands trailing over my hips and to my ass. His palms squeeze me hard enough that it teeters along that painful-pleasure line.

My clit brushes over his hard dick, and if we do this much longer, I'll be coming from dry-humping alone.

Like he can read my mind, he pulls back, dropping his forehead to mine.

"I've been imagining you in here with this thing almost nightly...and oftentimes in the shower. Hell, I can't even tell you the number of times the images have popped up when I'm doing something ridiculous like the dishes or something. I'd love to see if my fantasy matches the reality." Another squeeze. "If you're game, of course."

I don't know if I'm just that horny or if the thought of masturbating in front of him turns me on, but...

I roll off him, vibrator still in hand, and lie next to him.

I feel his eyes on me as I get comfortable, into the same position I would assume if I were doing this without an audience.

An audience... The thought of Dean watching me masturbate should probably scare me, make me nervous. But it doesn't.

I know how it feels to have his eyes on me when I do my yoga.

Him watching me masturbate? I'm getting wet just thinking about it.

I spread my legs and pull my panties to the side.

"You do it with your panties on?" I nod, and he gulps. "Holy fuck that's hot."

I chuckle. "It's lazy."

"No, River," he says, tossing the blanket completely off the bed and grabbing his cock. "It means you were so damn worked up you couldn't even bother taking your panties off. I promise you, that's hot as fuck."

When he says it like that...

I turn the toy on, and he chuckles.

"What?"

"Nothing." He shakes his head. "Just now I know what the buzzing I heard was."

My cheeks redden and I switch it back off, covering my face with my hands.

He pulls them back down. "No, no. Don't be embarrassed."

"How can I not be? You heard me masturbating!"

"Have you heard me take a shower before?"

"Yes?"

"Then you've heard me doing it too." He leans down and kisses me softly. "Now," he says, lips still resting on mine, "teach me what your body likes, River."

He takes my hands and guides them back between my legs. Except this time, it's him who pulls my panties to the side.

His throat bobs up and down when he looks at my pussy, and I've never felt so exposed and so fucking enthralled at the same time before.

The way he's looking at me like I'm some sort of gift... it's exhilarating.

He brushes his thumb over my clit and grins at me when I sigh.

"Touch yourself. Show me."

I turn the toy back on and guide it into place.

He doesn't move his hand, keeping my panties pushed to the side. Right away, all my senses light up and I gasp, loving the feel of his hands on me in combination with the toy.

Dean's lips part, watching the vibrator work its magic on my nerve endings. Slowly, he begins to stroke his cock, and I realize I could watch him do it every day for the rest of my life and never grow bored.

His eyes never leave me as I work the toy over my most sensitive area, my hips moving in time with the undulations. His tongue darts out to wet his drying lips, but his strokes never grow more hurried. He's genuinely enjoying watching me, and this moment is all about me.

On any given day, this toy can get me where I need to be in under five minutes.

Right now, it takes less than three.

I slam my eyes closed as my orgasm races through me, and I push my hips off the bed, chasing the high for as long as possible.

When all the aftershocks are gone, I switch the toy off and peel my eyes back open.

He's still holding my panties to the side. Still looking at my pussy. Still unwilling to take his eyes off me.

He's sweating, panting like he's the one who just came.

I lick my lips and swallow, trying to catch my breath.

"You good?"

He finally looks at me.

Hunger.

It's all I see in Dean's eyes.

"There's a very, *very* tiny part of me that wants to be offended you came so fast and so hard, but *holy fucking shit.*" He fits himself between my legs, caging my head in with his arms, dropping his mouth to mine. "That was the hottest thing I have ever witnessed, and I want to do it again."

"Now?"

He shakes his head. "No."

He slides down my body, shouldering his way between my legs. He pulls my underwear to the side, then gives me that devilish smirk I'm starting to love.

"I want a turn."

He disappears between my legs, and I fall into paradise.

I try to ignore the knowledge that this will all eventually disappear.

"I THOUGHT WE WERE FRIENDS."

I drag my eyes from the documents in front of me, looking at my best friend. She's leaning over the front counter of Making Waves, mindlessly drawing circles on the countertop.

"We are?"

"Yeah? Then why didn't you tell me you and Dean had sex?"

"W-What?" I sputter. "How did you know?"

"I didn't, but now I do." She beams, clapping her hands together and bouncing up and down. "Oh my *gosh*. I knew this day would come!"

I huff. "You suck, you know that?"

"I'm aware."

"How did you know?"

She lifts a slender shoulder. "A best friend just knows

these things. Plus, you have that *I just got fucked* glow about you. Man, I miss that glow."

She sighs longingly, and I'm sure she's thinking about the recent crumbling of her marriage to Sam's dad.

She shakes her head. "But never mind that. I have *so* many questions. When did it happen? How did it happen? Are you guys dating now? When are you getting married?"

"Settle down, you freak."

"I can't!" She squeals. "I'm just so excited for you. *Finally!*" More clapping. "I've waited so long for you two to wake up and realize you have feelings for each other."

"Feelings? Oh, no. There are no feelings."

She stops bouncing and pins me with those startling gray eyes of hers. "Are you seriously still denying it?"

"No, because there's nothing to deny. I do *not* have feelings for Dean."

"Are you trying to convince me or yourself?"

"You." When she doesn't stop staring like she's going to come over the counter at me, I stack the financial documents I was combing through, slip them back into their rightful folder, and toss it onto the counter. I rest my head on one hand. "What do you want to know?"

She mirrors my position. "You're not dating?"

"No."

"But you are sleeping together?"

"Yes."

"How many times have you had sex?"

"Four…and a half."

She gasps, excitement in her eyes. "When?"

"It started two nights ago."

"And?"

I know what she's asking even without her saying it.

I do everything to hold back my sigh as I think about the way Dean is in bed.

He's attentive. Demanding, yet gentle. Rough in all the right ways.

"It's incredible."

"You lucky dog." She pouts. "The only reason I'm not jealous is because I've sworn off dick."

"Because of the dick you were married to."

"Precisely." She nods, pushing away from the counter. "How'd it happen?"

"Well…" I draw out. "He kissed me on Sunday. We didn't really discuss it at first, but the tension was there, you know? It just all sort of came to a head and…" I motion with my hand. "Here we are."

"So, if you're not dating but you're sleeping together, you're…what? Friends with benefits?"

"We're not labeling it. It's just something fun to pass the time and relieve some stress."

She tilts her head, pursing her lips, studying me. "Hmm."

Uh-oh. I know that *hmm*.

That *hmm* means she has something to say but doesn't want to say it.

"What?"

"It's just…" she starts, and I called that right. That's how she *always* starts the *hmm*s. "Do you think that's a good idea?"

"Which part?"

"All of it. Aren't you worried it'll get all…confusing? Worried you'll fall for him?"

Me fall for Dean? Ha!

"No." I shake my head. "We're adults. We can keep it casual."

Another head tilt.

"What." This time it doesn't come out as a question. I'm starting to get annoyed.

"Do you like him?"

"I mean, I let him see me naked, so I have to like him on some level, right?"

She frowns at my answer. "You know what I mean, River."

"Do I have a tiny—and I mean *tiny*—crush on Dean? Yes. Am I going to do anything about it? No. It's not going to go anywhere. He'll be moving out once his apartment is done and we'll go back to being neighbors. This is just temporary. We're on the same page with this."

"He's your neighbor. It's not like him moving out would be a long-distance relationship."

"Ah," I say. "That's just it—he lives next door, so if things go south with us, I'll have to continue living next to him or move, and I love my apartment. I'd much rather take my chances of it being a smidge awkward knowing we've seen each other naked than feelings getting involved and us having to navigate that. You know what I mean?"

She heaves a sigh. "Yeah, I can understand that. It's just... be careful, you know? I don't want you getting hurt."

"I'm a big girl, Maya. I'll be fine."

I hope.

Chapter 16

DEAN

"YOU COULD HAVE AT LEAST TOLD me you were inviting someone over. I would have, I don't know, put a damn bra on."

"Don't look at her tits." I point to my best friend, who is still standing in the doorway, a six-pack of beer in one hand. "River, meet Nolan. Come on in, man."

He sticks his free hand out. "We've briefly met before, but it's nice to officially meet you. Sorry he's an idiot and didn't tell you I was coming over."

Shaking his hand, she glares at me.

I shrug. "What? I wanted someone else to watch the game with for a change."

"I wasn't that bad."

"Weren't you though?"

I can tell she wants to argue, but she knows I'm right.

Just two nights ago she came home to find me on the couch watching a game. She didn't even change out of her work clothes, just flopped down on the couch, ate no less than ten wings, and forced me to explain the entire sport to her.

I'll never tell her this, but it was my favorite game I've ever watched.

"I'll just go work in my office or something. I have a couple things I can take care of while you stare at other guys' butts."

"I just want to go on record saying I will not be staring at other guys' butts. I don't even like baseball," Nolan says.

"So you'd be looking at the butts if they weren't attached to the players?" she teases him.

His eyes widen, panicked.

"Leave him alone, River," I tell her. "Go work."

"I'm going, I'm going—but only because I *do* have a lot of work to do and not because I'm letting you boss me around. I just don't want to be around you anymore."

"What'd I tell you about your shortness and that sass of yours? There's too little of you and too much of it."

She scowls. "I hate you."

"Liar."

Spinning on her heel, she turns to Nolan. "I won't tell anyone you watch for the butts. I know that's why I endure it."

He laughs. "I appreciate that."

She turns her angry eyes on me once more before stomping off down the hall.

I can't wipe the goofy smile off my face as I watch her sashay away.

When she disappears into her room, I turn to Nolan, and he raises his brow.

"What?" I say, grabbing the six-pack from his hand.

"Nothing. I like her, man. She's feisty."

"If by feisty you mean annoying, then yes." I motion for him to follow me into the apartment. "First pitch was already thrown. I put the wings in the oven to warm 'em up. I'll pop these in the fridge."

I take off for the kitchen and Nolan heads for the living room.

"'Sup, shithead?" I hear him say to Leo.

He made so much fun of me for taking the little guy home at first, but he's grown attached to him like I have.

I slide all but two beers into the fridge and check on the wings. I'm on my way to the living room when River's bedroom door opens. I stop in my tracks when she walks out.

Arching a single brow, she lifts her shirt, flashing me her tits.

She drops her top, blows me a kiss, and hurries into the office like nothing happened.

I fight to not drop the beers, scoop her into my arms, and show her there are consequences for acting like that.

Fucking tease.

Morris barrels past me and into the room, running straight to Nolan as he takes a seat on the couch.

To my surprise, Morris jumps right into Nolan's lap, curling into a ball like he belongs there.

"Cats love me," he explains with a shrug, running his hand through the cat's white fluff. He looks around the apartment. "I can see why you agreed to stay here. This place is way nicer than yours." Nolan grabs the beer I hand him and cracks the top open. "Thanks, man."

I settle down at the other end of the couch, popping open my own drink. "It's the exact same apartment, just flipped."

"Yeah, but this one is...*homier.* You didn't have a single picture hanging up in your place and hardly any furniture. It felt...cold. Boring." He takes a drink of his beer, turning his attention to the game on the TV.

He has a point.

I never noticed how lonely my apartment felt until I started staying with River. It was the small things, like those silly knickknacks shaped like s'mores she has on the shelves, or the many throw pillows she has piled up on the couch. Even the lone piece of art she has hanging above the TV is enough to make it feel more like a home and not just someplace to crash.

I didn't realize how empty my life was before...and I don't just mean in the literal sense.

Living with River this past month has been absolutely fucking exhausting at times. She's moody thanks to her insomnia, she's opinionated, and there's a certain way she likes things done, which is hard to get a handle on sometimes.

But then there are all the moments in between.

She's funny. Whip-smart. One of the hardest-working people I've ever met. She's caring and dedicated to the people in her life. And as much as she frustrates me, she intrigues me.

For the first time in a long time, I'm not looking to fill my life with activities. I'm good with just existing in this space with her. I don't bother trying to stick around and talk with other teachers at summer school, and I no longer find myself scrolling my phone at the gym long after my workout session is over. I just want to race home and be with her.

It scares me, considering our arrangement and how temporary it is.

But it also makes me wonder how it would be if we gave this thing between us a real shot...

I relax into the couch and try not to think too much about things I shouldn't be thinking about. I take a long pull of my beer.

"So, when did you start sleeping together?"

Beer bubbles back up, dribbling out of my mouth and down my chin.

I wipe the mess with the back of my hand, and Nolan laughs.

"What the fuck, dude?"

"Sorry, not sorry." He shrugs. "So, when did it start up?"

I glance toward the hall, making sure River is still tucked safely inside the bedroom where she can't hear our conversation.

"What makes you think we're sleeping together?" I ask when I'm sure the coast is clear. I keep my voice low though, just in case.

He gives me a *Don't bullshit me* look. "For one, you're happier. That means one of two things: your sports-ball team is kicking some serious ass, or you're getting your dick sucked frequently."

"Jesus, Nolan."

"Just Nolan is fine," he says.

I shake my head at him, and he lifts a questioning brow.

I roll my eyes. "About two weeks ago." I take another drink of my beer. "But it's just sex."

He grins, feeling damn proud of himself, I'm sure. "I fucking knew it."

"You didn't know shit."

"Did too. You usually talk my ear off about this broad, but suddenly you were all clammed up. I've known you a long damn time, Dean. When you're not vocal about what you're doing, it means you know you shouldn't be doing it."

"I shouldn't be sleeping with her?"

"No, man, you definitely should—you two have danced around it long enough. It's that friends-with-benefits, just-sex bullshit you're feeding each other that you know you shouldn't be doing."

"Dude, I'm telling you, it's just—"

"Sex. Oh, I heard you. I just don't believe you."

"Why the fuck not?"

"Because it's never just sex for you."

"I've had casual sex before," I argue.

"Sure, but not with anyone you actually give a shit about. There's a big difference between the two."

"I—"

Fuck. He has a point.

I'm so tired of him having points.

I've known River for a year now. In that time, we've been neighbors, enemies, roommates, and now lovers. It's like once the lines started to blur on what we were, we gave up and jumped in full force.

What we're doing is dumb, there's no denying that.

But not doing it doesn't feel right either.

Because as much as I don't want to, I like River.

Her.

Not just her body or the way she feels falling apart around me.

Though I don't want to think about it too much or admit it, I'm going to have a hard time walking away from this when it's time to go our separate ways.

Nolan grins. "You like her, don't you?"

"I wouldn't be sleeping with her if I didn't."

"You know what I mean."

I groan, tossing my head back and running a hand through my hair, frustrated with myself.

It's a way to relieve tension and that's it. Nothing more.

That's all it is. All it's supposed to be.

So why do I feel myself beginning to want more with her? I haven't been interested in a relationship with anyone in a long time. Why the fuck do I suddenly feel like it might not be a crazy idea with River, of all people?

I swear I'm going crazy.

"Does she know?" Nolan asks.

He can tell I like her. He doesn't have to hear me say it to know.

"No. I'm like ninety-five percent sure she still hates my guts. This is all just sex for her."

He laughs lightly, turning back to the TV. "Trust me, she doesn't hate you. She wishes she did, but she doesn't."

Fuck me if I don't hope he's right.

"DO you always have to hog the bed?"

"Last I checked, it's *my* bed—I can hog it all I want." She shoves at me, trying to force me out, but I'm too heavy. "Why are you even still in here?"

"Because my bed is an air mattress, that's why."

And because you sleep better when I'm in here.

I've stayed in River's bed almost every night since we started sleeping together. Mostly because we're always fucking or fooling around, but also because it's become increasingly obvious that she sleeps better when I'm here. The few nights I didn't stay over, I woke up to her on the air mattress beside me.

"That's your own fault," she says, still shoving and getting nowhere.

Accepting defeat with a huff, she abandons her mission. She reaches over to the nightstand on her side, grabbing her laptop and pulling it over into her lap.

The glow from the screen illuminates her face, and she looks so fucking cute when she's concentrating.

A wrinkle forms between her brows and she twists her bottom lip in her fingers. Her long red locks are piled in a messy bun on top of her head, and she's wearing her standard bedtime attire of a camisole and panties.

I keep trying to convince her to try sleeping naked like me, but she won't budge on it.

"Working this late?" I ask.

"The grind never stops." She taps the keyboard a few times. "Our online store is doing *really* well, and I'm getting more items added to the website to meet demands. Plus, I've been a little distracted lately and I've fallen behind. Or at least *my* version of behind."

"You're very passionate about your work."

She peeks down at me, and it's clear she's going on the defense.

I hold my hands up. "I don't mean any offense by that. Truly. Your work ethic is inspiring. A little worrisome that you don't take more time to shut off and step away, but still inspiring."

Her eyes spark with surprise and something else I can't quite decipher.

"Thank you," she murmurs. "That's...well, I like hearing that from you."

From you.

I don't know why those two words hit differently, but they do.

They feel...intimate.

That feeling from before, the one that made my chest feel all weird...it's back.

"You're welcome." I clear my throat, rubbing at the spot. "Have you always been such a workaholic?"

She twists her lips up, thinking.

"No," she decides. "Believe it or not, I actually used to be fun. I guess I just buried my loneliness in work and it stuck. The business has been booming, and I'm hitting goals I always dreamed of." She shrugs. "So I just never let up."

I want to ask if she's still feeling lonely, or if she's behind on work because she's no longer hiding behind it. I want to know if that's my doing or something else.

But that feels too much like crossing a line.

"I can relate. What's that saying? Find something you love and never work a day in your life?"

"That saying is horseshit." I laugh at her brashness. "Just because it comes from a place of love and passion doesn't mean it doesn't take hard work."

"True. I'm passionate about teaching, but it's exhausting as hell."

"Why'd you go into it exactly? You worked for your dad before you got your degree, right? What went wrong there?"

I wince, not a fan of explaining this part of my life to people. "So. Funny story."

"People are never about to tell a funny story when they say that."

"True." I roll onto my back, putting my hands under my head. I don't miss the way her eyes trail down my body when the blanket slips down to my hips. "My parents won the lottery and my dad started a business with the winnings."

"Like legit won the lottery?"

"Yep."

"So you're loaded?"

I laugh. "How much do you think teachers get paid?"

"But your parents…"

"*They* have money. Holland makes good cash working for my father, but since I ditched the family business and all, I'm on my own."

"They cut you off?"

"There wasn't anything to cut off. We grew up scraping by, and when they struck gold, my parents were adamant that aside from a good education, if we didn't help keep the wealth flowing, we were on our own."

"That seems…"

"A little ass-backward considering they got everything handed to them? Yeah." I shrug. "But it's fine. I'm not into the whole glitz-and-glam lifestyle they've adopted. I'm more into the low-key thing."

"Ah, spoken like a true broke man."

I chuckle. "And you? How was your home life?"

"Nothing exciting. Parents are still together. No real drama. Picket fence and all that crap." She lifts a shoulder. "I grew up about thirty minutes away. I went off to college for a while, and when I moved back, I knew I wanted to live in the city." She gestures around the room. "So, here I am. Nothing to write home about."

"I don't think that's true," I say quietly. "There's a lot to write about when it comes to you."

Her lips pull at the corners, and if it weren't for the laptop light, I'd miss the grin.

I close my eyes, listening to her fingers clack against the keyboard.

"What about you?" she asks when I think she's completely focused on other things.

"What about me?"

"Do you ever hide in your work? Ever feel lonely?"

I didn't. Not until this. Not until I realized what I might be missing.

"Not anymore," I say.

She nods once but doesn't look at me.

I fall asleep trying not to overthink the idea that tonight is the first time I've slept in here without the preface of sex… and what that might mean.

Chapter 17

RIVER

"I SWEAR, if I miss the cherry pie because of you, I'm going to be—"

"What?" Dean cuts me off. "Big mad?" I shoot daggers at him when he throws my words back at me, but he ignores me. "*You* were the one who insisted on getting dirty again after our showers."

"That was one hundred percent your fault."

"I'm sorry, did I *make* you suck my cock?"

I blush at his crassness.

I simply couldn't help myself. He stepped out of the bathroom in nothing but a towel, the water tracking down his abs.

I just wanted to see where it landed is all.

Sue me.

"What the hell!" I smack at him, peeking around the sidewalk as we speed-walk toward the diner to make Sunday breakfast, making sure nobody heard us. "You can't just say something like that, especially in public."

"Or what?"

"Or…or…I'll snuff you!"

"Snuff me?" He pulls open the door to The Gravy Train. "What are you, a mobster?"

"Guess you won't know until you know," I say, slipping past him and into the diner.

He doesn't look the least bit scared.

We step into the line that's already formed at the ordering counter, and I don't miss the way Dean doesn't remove his hand from the small of my back.

"Seriously, Dean, if they're out of cherry pie…"

He moves toward me, cutting off my words as he pushes his body against mine. Warmth seeps into me, and beads of sweat begin to form on my neck.

I want to sweep my hair into a bun to help cool down, but I can't. Dean's hands are on my hips, squeezing me in a teasing manner. The five o'clock shadow he's always sporting tickles my face as he bends down, bringing his lips to my ear.

"If they're out of cherry, I'll make it up to you."

"Make it up to me?"

I feel him nod. "I'll let you suck my cock again."

I clench my thighs.

We've been sleeping together for three weeks now, and I'm still not used to the dirty words that fall from his lips.

I'm not sure I'll ever get used to them…or over them.

"Stop it!" I hiss.

His grip tightens on me, pulling my body flush with his.

There's no mistaking what I'm feeling.

He's getting hard.

In the middle of the diner.

Right out in the open.

I take a deep breath and try to step away, but he doesn't let me.

"Don't even think about moving."

I don't.

"Then stop teasing."

"Fine, but only because your best friend and her kid just walked in." He waves to Maya, beaming at her. "Hey, guys."

"You're running late today," she comments, eyeing us, not missing how close we're standing. "Hope they still have cherry pie for you."

"I hope they don't," Dean says, and I fall into a coughing fit, picking up on his double entendre.

I elbow him in the stomach, and he grunts, rubbing at the spot I hit, finally shifting away from me.

I welcome the space and miss his warmth all at the same time.

I gather my long hair into my hand, picking it up off my neck and wrapping it into a messy bun.

"Hey, Sam," I say to my nephew.

He grunts, not looking up from the phone in his hands.

Maya rolls her eyes. "Pre-teens."

"Choir," Dean tells her, pointing to himself.

She shakes her head. "Still don't know how you do it."

"Lots and lots of whiskey and pie." He nods toward our usual table. "Why don't you two go grab our spot? Sam and I can manage this. Right, Sam?"

Another eloquent grunt from him.

"Don't forget my cherry," I say to Dean over my shoulder as Maya and I head to the table.

"Oh, yeah. I'll get right on that."

He winks at me, and I grin.

"Please tell me that wasn't some kind of sex code," she says as we grab our favorite seats.

"It wasn't."

"Liar."

I giggle, and she smiles at me.

"You know, as much as I'm a little wary of your *laissez-faire* attitude about this thing you two are doing, I love seeing you smile so much. It's been a long time since you've been happy."

"I've always been happy."

She shakes her head. "Not *this* kind of happy. It's...different."

It *feels* different.

I feel different.

"I've just been getting more sleep," I tell her, which isn't a lie.

I *have* been sleeping well. My insomnia isn't gone, because that's not how insomnia works, but having Dean there at night helps calm my worries and ease my mind. He gives me something to focus on other than my racing thoughts.

More than that, for the first time in a long time, I don't *want* to focus just on work and hide behind it.

I want to live in the moment...with him.

"Even with your sex schedule?" she teases. "Lucky bitch."

We laugh, giggling like fools, drawing the attention of a few other customers, including Dean.

When he lifts a brow, I wave him off, and he shrugs, turning back to Sam. They're talking and carrying on like old friends, and I love how he's able to draw Sam out of his shell. How he talks to him and relates to him on a level nobody else seems to.

"It's Dean, you know," Maya says.

I know it is.

She doesn't have to tell me that.

He makes me laugh as much as he drives me crazy. Makes my body vibrate in all the right ways just as much as he does the wrong ones.

How can you loathe someone so much and still feel this good because of them?

Maybe you don't loathe him at all...

I silence that voice that keeps popping up in my head.

I *have* to hate him.

If I don't, I just might have to admit that maybe...just maybe...I never hated him at all.

And we promised no pressure, no plans for the future. This is *just* to relieve the tension.

"Good news." Dean sets two plates on the table. "I was able to score some pie."

"Bad news," Sam adds. "It's not cherry."

"Did you seriously enlist my child to deliver the bad news to take the heat off you?" Maya glares at Dean accusingly.

"Yes."

I snicker at his answer as he slides into the seat next to me, his arm brushing against mine.

"Sorry about that cherry pie, River."

Heat creeps up my cheeks, and I dare a peek over at him.

He gives me a wolfish grin, bouncing his brows up and down.

I snap my attention back to my pie, shoving a forkful of gooey deliciousness into my mouth in order to refrain from leaning over and kissing him.

"Okay, wow." Maya wags her finger between the two of us. "I like you two together. This dynamic is...wow."

"Dean is your boyfriend, Aunt River?"

I pause mid-bite. Maya's eyes widen, her mouth dropping open as she realizes what she just did.

Sorry, she mouths.

I rack my brain, trying to figure out how to answer this.

"I—"

"Yep," Dean says. "That cool?"

Sam grins, nodding. "Totally."

They go on talking like nothing happened. Like my heart isn't hammering in my chest. Like it's not going to explode over one word.

Yep.

He said it so easily. So calmly.

So sure.

And it felt so…right.

Why did it feel so right?

Maya's foot brushes against my shin. I look up at her, and she tips her head, silently asking if I'm okay.

I shrug.

Because I don't know if I am okay.

And I don't know how to handle that.

Maya's cell starts vibrating in her purse and she digs around, trying to find it.

I take the opportunity to slip away.

"I'll be right back," I mutter, pushing up from the stool and rushing to the bathroom without looking back at the table.

I lean against the door and inhale several deep breaths.

I'm overwhelmed. Confused. Excited.

Disappointed.

Not in Dean's answer, but because it wasn't real.

Why am I disappointed it wasn't real? What the hell is happening?

There's a knock on the door.

"Occupied!" I call.

"No shit. Open up."

It's Dean.

And for the first time in weeks, I don't want to see him.

"No."

"River, I will bust this door down. I can do it and you know it. Let me in."

With a defeated sigh, I flip the lock.

He pushes the door open, slipping inside and putting the lock back in place.

He turns to me, his eyes sharp and worried. "Is everything okay? You just kind of disappeared out there."

"Yeah. Everything's good," I lie.

He narrows his eyes. "I don't believe you."

"Well," I say, plastering on a saucy smile, "that's too bad. But now that I have you alone…"

I grab the collar of his shirt, dragging him down for a kiss, silencing all the questions and doubt running through my mind.

His big hands go to my hips instantly, and he pulls me tightly against him. He's already getting hard, and I almost have to wonder if the man is always walking around half-cocked.

He walks me backward until I bump into the sink. With little effort, he picks me up and sets me on the counter, stepping between my legs. The skirt I'm wearing is scrunched around my waist, and I can feel the cool air hit my already heated core.

There's no half-cocked about it.

Dean's hard.

His erection brushes against my pussy, and I moan.

Hands slide up my neck and into my hair, pulling the messy bun free. He twines his fingers through the wavy red locks, playing with the strands like they're his guitar strings.

He pulls his mouth away, panting, and presses his forehead against mine.

"You're killing me."

"Same."

"We shouldn't be doing this here."

"We shouldn't," I agree. "But…"

"But…"

His lips find mine again, and we're lost in another heated kiss, mouths moving together in a passionate storm.

Someone knocks on the door, and we ignore it, completely lost in one another.

I don't know who comes up for air first, but we're both gasping for it.

"Maya."

"What?" he asks, confused.

"Maya—she's out there waiting for us."

He shakes his head. "She left. That was her ex-husband calling—family emergency with his mother or something."

"Oh."

His eyes turn two shades darker. "*Oh*."

Like we can read the other's mind, we move at the same time.

He works to unbuckle his jeans and I shove my panties down my legs.

He crushes his mouth to mine and slips his hand between my legs, sliding a finger inside me. Then two.

Next he's yanking me to the edge of the counter and sinking into me with one deep thrust.

He swallows my moans with his mouth, slamming into me over and over.

Fucking me hard. *Fast.*

Until I'm no longer scared or worried.

Until I stop thinking about the fact that I don't hate Dean Evans.

And I start to fall.

Chapter 18

DEAN

"I CANNOT BELIEVE you brought your damn turtle to a roller derby game."

"I can't believe you can't believe it." I set Leo's on-the-go hut on the chair next to mine. "He's been looking lonely lately. With all the rain we've been having, I haven't had the chance to get him to the park. He needs some action."

"I thought turtles were loners."

"Some are, but since he grew up with people, he's pretty used to them and doesn't spook too easily. He's more curious than anything." I tap the hut with my knuckle, and he bumps his nose against it. "Plus, look how cute he is. Do you really think I can leave him in his terrarium all the time?"

"You're so strange," she mutters.

"You like my strange."

"That's about the only thing I like about you."

"Oh, I have it on good authority that's not true." I put my lips to her ear, and she shivers at the contact. "You like my abs. My mouth. My co—"

She covers said mouth with her hand, and I laugh, pulling it away.

"Cooking skills," I finish.

"First of all, cooking and *you know what* don't even have the same vowel sound—you're reaching. Second, I know better than anyone your cooking skills are trash." Her red hair bounces as she shakes her head.

"Too soon, River. Too soon."

I was worried last week at The Gravy Train that something had shifted between us, but everything fell back into place when we walked out of the bathroom.

Something was bothering her when she went in though, and I'd bet money it was me telling Sam we're dating. Thing is, I was backed into a corner and had to cover with something. River's mood shifted the moment I said I was her boyfriend.

I'm not sure if she was upset that I said it, or if she wanted it to be true.

Either answer has me sweating.

My insurance agent called this morning to let me know my apartment will be finished next week, about two weeks sooner than expected. On one hand, I'm glad to be done with this fire fiasco so soon. But I'd be lying if I said I wasn't bummed my time with River is being cut short.

Looks like the clock on this game we're playing is winding down, and we're nearing the final buzzer.

The craziest part? I want to keep playing.

I just have no idea which team River's on.

"I have literally zero idea about this sport," she says, flipping through the program. "You're going to have to explain it."

"Your guess is going to be as good as mine. I'm a roller derby virgin."

"Don't worry," Caroline says in front of us. "I'll have

Cooper explain it to you when he gets back with snacks. He loves it."

"Coop is here? Thank fuck. Thought I was going to have to endure spending *another* night alone with River."

"Hey!"

"I'm kidding, I'm kidding." I throw my arm around her shoulders, but she shoves me off.

"Don't touch me," she says.

"Uh-huh. Just remember that later when you're begging me to do just the opposite."

A giggle comes from behind us and I peek at who's listening in.

It's the woman from the elevator, the one who said she always knew we'd get together. I still can't remember her name.

"Such a cute couple." She grins. "When did you two start dating?"

"Uh…" I scratch at my stubble.

It's one thing to tell a twelve-year-old we're dating for the sake of not explaining the term FWB, but it's another to use the same lie with someone else.

That starts to make the lie a whole lot more real.

"A little over a month ago now," River answers.

I raise a brow at her, and she shrugs with a grin.

About ten people around us, most from our building and a few from the diner, mumble and grumble. Someone sitting three seats down whoops with delight.

"Pay up, suckers!"

Caroline spins around in her chair, scowling at us. "You two just cost me fifty bucks."

Money starts changing hands, everyone forking it over to

the little old lady sitting at the end. It's Mailbox Betty, a nickname earned for always sitting around the mailboxes snooping on packages and eavesdropping on conversations. Everyone in the building knows she's the gossip queen.

"I told you all!" She collects the cash coming her way. "I had a hunch."

"A hunch? You're just a nosy old bat!" someone shouts from two rows to the left behind us.

"Uh, what the hell is going on?" River asks, looking around the crowd. "Caroline?"

She winces, her cartoon-like blue eyes filled with terror and remorse. "Funny story…"

I snicker, remembering what River said about that phrase.

"There was sort of a…pool going on," Caroline continues. "In the building and at the diner."

"A pool?"

"Like a giant betting pool," I say. I sit back, crossing my arms with an amused grin. "You dicks have been betting on our relationship status, haven't you?"

Several of them bob their heads up and down.

I laugh.

Of course they would.

"What!" River explodes, shooting up from her chair. "You guys have seriously been *betting* on us?" More nods. "That is messed up on *so* many levels." She turns her heated gaze on Caroline. "And you knew? *Participated?*"

She has the decency to look ashamed. "The winning pot could pay an entire month's rent."

"You are *so* fired!" River says.

Caroline's jaw drops, and I shake my head. "No you're not."

221

"Shut up, Dean. She is too." She motions toward the other gamblers. "And ha! The joke is on all of you because we aren't dating. We're just friends with benefits."

Several people exchange glances, all looking at each other to see if anyone had that piece of information.

Then one by one, they all fall into fits of laughter.

"Oh, honey," Mailbox Betty says, swiping at her eyes. "What you two are is *not* friends with benefits. You're dating."

"No we're not!" River argues back. "We are definitely *not* dating."

I bristle at the hardness in her voice. Like she can't even fathom someone suggesting such a thing in a serious capacity. Like dating me would be the worst thing in the world.

Guess now I don't have to worry—she clearly doesn't feel the same as I do about keeping this going.

That peculiar ache returns, and I rub at my chest, trying to get it to go away.

Several people give us a sad smile at River's continued insistence. A few people put their heads together, whispering and pointing.

Okay then…

A pair of skates skid into my peripheral as Lucy skates to a stop in front of us. She removes her mouthguard, her hands going to her hips.

"Who won?" she asks.

"Lucy!" River admonishes. "You too?"

Our building manager grins. "Who do you think organized it?"

I laugh, and it gains River's attention.

"Please do not tell me *you're* in on it too. Tell me this is not some version of *She's All That* or something where the hot guy gets the dorky chick to sleep with him all for a bet."

"First, I'm so happy to hear you think I'm hot. Second, no, I'm not in on this. I'm just as surprised as you." I glance around the group. "And flattered you all care about my sex life so much."

A few of them snicker.

River drops back down into her chair. "Assholes. The whole lot of them."

"Just some harmless fun," Lucy says, tapping her skate against River's foot. "We don't mean anything by it, dear, though I am glad you two finally got together."

"But we—"

"Oh, just give it a rest and accept it already, River," Caroline pipes up. I'm surprised because she's typically so shy and quiet. "You're sleeping together and living together. You do everything together, include annoy the rest of us with your *will they, won't they* schtick. Just call it what it is: you're dating."

"For the record, I'm with her," Lucy says. She looks at me. "Heard the good news about your apartment. You excited to get back in there?"

River freezes next to me.

Fuck.

I plaster on a false smile for Lucy. "Yep. I can't wait."

She nods, grinning back at me, but her smile doesn't quite reach her eyes. "Good. That's…good. Well, I better get to reffing. The game is about to start. I appreciate you coming out to see this old lady skate in a bunch of circles."

She taps River's foot again, drawing her attention.

"You're not alone in your feelings."

With a wink, she glides off to the center of the rink.

"What was that?" I ask.

River shrugs, staring after Lucy, face twisted in confusion. "I have no clue."

"Huh."

"Hey, guys," Cooper says, sliding in between the seats. "What'd I miss?"

Caroline hitches her thumb over her shoulder. "You owe Mailbox Betty fifty bucks."

WE'VE BARELY SAID ten sentences to each other since Lucy dropped the news that my apartment is almost done.

On one hand, I'm glad River's quiet about it. I don't have to hear if she's excited or not that I'm leaving

And on the other, it makes me absolutely fucking *insane*.

"You were going to tell me, right?" She rolls over to face me, peering up at me with round eyes. "About your apartment. You were going to tell me before you left?"

"No. I was just going to pack my shit and leave."

Her jaw drops, and I laugh.

"Yes, River. Of course I was going to tell you. Why wouldn't I?"

"It would be...I don't know." She lifts a shoulder. "Awkward? We said we wanted to avoid that."

We said a lot of things, like no attachments.

I fucked that one up royally.

I've grown way too comfortable over here in the past month. Going back to my apartment is going to be hard, probably harder than I thought.

It's not going to be harder than moving past this thing we're doing and pretending nothing happened.

But if that's what River wants…

I lift my hand to her shoulder and drag my fingertips down her arm in slow, sweet strokes. Her skin pebbles under my touch, and I can see her nipples do too. "We did say that, but I guess I'd hope you know me better by now. After…everything."

"Everything," she repeats quietly.

I've been with River for over a month now, seen parts of her I only dreamed of seeing.

But this moment?

It's the most naked we've been.

Lying in the quiet room, nothing between us but a sheet.

"When?"

It's whispered, so low I almost don't hear it.

"Next week," I tell her.

She exhales slowly, then nods.

Leaning forward, she lays her lips against mine. Not kissing me, just resting them there as she pushes me onto my back. She swings her leg over my hip, straddling me.

My cock brushes against the heat between her legs, and the desire I always seem to have for her swells to life.

"Then we better make it count, Dean."

And we do.

Chapter 19

RIVER

I DID something today I haven't done in the entire five years I've owned Making Waves.

I called in sick.

Caroline was understanding, and I despised the pity in her voice. I almost got dressed and went in to work just to spite her because of it.

Instead, I've been planted on the couch all day watching crap TV shows I don't give a shit about.

It's been almost one week since Dean left and since I've seen him, even though he still lives next door.

I was a complete coward on the morning of his move. I ran off to work early to avoid the inevitable awkwardness and made sure to get home extra late when I knew he'd be long gone.

Now, after a week without a glimpse of him, the regret is sinking in like a stone. Has my stomach all twisted up in knots.

Knuckles rap against my door, and my heart flutters with anticipation.

Dean.

"River." Maya's voice floats through the door.

Not Dean.

Great. Caroline must have told her I didn't come in.

I know I need to answer, or she'll stand out there all day, and I don't need to risk her running into Dean.

With reluctance, I peel myself off the couch, trying to ignore the missing terrarium as I pass the console, and pull open the front door.

Her eyes rake over me as she assesses my state with a frown.

I'm aware I'm wearing my standard "breakup outfit"—my joggers and my t-shirt with a bunch of holes in it—even though we didn't technically break up.

We were never together, so how could we?

"I told you."

I sigh, walking away from the door as she follows me inside.

"I don't want to hear your *I told you so* stuff, Maya. I love you like a sister, but I will slap you."

"Eh, I could take you. I have before."

"It was *one* fight, and you were pregnant. I couldn't hit you!"

"A win is a win." She laughs. "I brought pie. It's not cherry, but it is Dutch apple."

"Just set it on the counter. I'm not hungry."

She disappears into the kitchen, then comes back and takes a seat on the edge of the couch where I've curled back up.

"You look awful."

"Gee, thanks. I really needed a kick when I'm already down." She tries to push my hair out of my face, and I swat her hand away. "Stop it. I'm fine."

"You don't look fine. You look heartbroken."

"That'll happen when you get your heart broken."

She purses her lips. "How can you be heartbroken if you weren't dating?"

I don't say anything.

A sly smile slides across her face.

"You love him. You're *in love* with him."

"Me in love with Dean? Please. I—OUCH!"

She whacks me *hard* on the ass.

"What the hell, Maya?" I cry out, rubbing my already aching butt cheek.

"Does that hurt?" I nod. "Good. Now get off it and go tell your idiotic neighbor you're in love with him."

Her words sound crazy.

But in my heart, no matter how much I try to deny it, I know they're true.

As much as I don't want to be, I'm in love with Dean Evans.

For all the reasons I shouldn't be in love with him, I have ten more why I should.

He annoys me, but he makes me laugh just as much. We argue too much, but he challenges me. We hardly have anything in common, but I always have fun with him. I want to be around him as much as I don't. He's kind, he's smart. Driven and funny.

And he's somehow managed to completely capture my heart.

I rub at where she hit me. "You just smacked my ass— likely left a damn welt—all for a joke?"

"No. Your ass just happened to be there, and it's pretty damn smackable."

She winks, and a smile slips through my anger.

I shake my head. "You bitch."

"You'll live…but only if you get up and talk to him."

"Maya, I love you—I really do—but I can't just waltz over there and be like, *Hey, I love you.*"

"And why the hell not?"

"Because he doesn't feel the same way," I mutter, looking anywhere but at her.

"What makes you say that?"

I wave a hand around my sad, lonely apartment. "He didn't stay. That's my first indication."

"Did you ask him to stay?"

Well…no.

But I knew he wouldn't. He had no reason to. We agreed. Once his apartment was done, we were done.

Him staying would mean we got attached.

We weren't supposed to get attached.

Tell that to my heart.

"You didn't, so you don't actually know if he would have." She laughs sardonically. "You two… I swear…" She pinches the bridge of her nose. "Dean loves you. I'd bet you an entire year's worth of cherry pie from The Gravy Train that man is head over heels for you."

In what world does she think Dean is in love with me?

We've been at each other's throat since the day he moved in. Morris snuck out and into his apartment. He was *such* a dick when he brought him home.

We haven't gotten along for a single day after that. There is absolutely *no way* he's secretly in love with me.

I move my head in the negative. "No way."

"Yes way. *Everyone* sees it but you two for some reason.

Me, Caroline, Lucy…we all do. Everyone but you."

"Tell me, what do you see that I don't?"

"For starters, there are your asinine reasons for loathing him. They're obvious cover-ups for lust."

"They—"

She holds her hand up. "Then there's the way that no matter what, no matter how many insults you throw at him or how many times you scowl at him, you still have his sole focus in a room." She grins. "I remember one time it was pouring rain outside. You were getting soaked, trying to walk as fast as your little legs would carry you to the diner, but it just wasn't fast enough."

"Sam came out with an umbrella for me."

She smiles. "That was all Dean. He saw you coming and knew you'd refuse any help from him, so he shoved an umbrella in Sam's hands and sent him out to rescue you."

That was…Dean?

I remember that day. I was so thankful I bought Sam ice cream every day for a week straight. The little twerp.

"And let's not forget all the times he's bought you pie."

"Stolen my pie, you mean."

"And bought it too. I picked up early on that he was paying for it and just let it happen. I wanted to smack him every time he got you all worked up over stealing your pie and you'd yell at him, but he'd never confess what he'd been doing." She rolls her eyes. "Then there are all the times he's come to the shop for gifts for his mom and sister."

"Dean shops at the boutique?"

"Oh yeah." She chuckles. "Often, actually. Christmas, birthdays, anniversary gifts. He's dropped a good amount of cash in there."

"I haven't once seen him in there."

"Because he knows you'd kick him out. He always makes sure to shop when you're not there."

I…I can't believe all this.

What else is Dean behind? And what does it all mean?

Nothing. Because he's not here now.

"I'm telling you, River, he's in love with you…though I'm not even sure he realizes it either."

She's wrong.

Just because he does things for me, that doesn't mean he loves me. It just means he's nice, and maybe a bit of a masochist.

"Look," Maya says, pushing up to her feet. "I just wanted to come check on you and bring you pie. I need to get back to work. My boss is kind of a hard-ass, and I don't want to get in trouble."

She frowns when I don't even smile at her joke.

With a sigh, she pats me on the shoulder and makes her way to the door.

When I hear the knob twist, I peek over at her.

"Tell him, River."

Then, she's gone.

I lie here for another half hour before surging to my feet and hitting the shower.

I need a distraction.

Something to keep my mind off this feeling. Need to bury myself in work, right back to the hilt, just like before when I didn't have the chance to sit around worrying about my love life.

Anything to keep me from thinking about Dean.

Chapter 20

DEAN

I HATE IT HERE.

I glance around my empty apartment with a heavy feeling in my gut.

I don't dislike it just because I'm practically starting from nothing and there's nothing inside.

It's everything else that's wrong.

Nothing is where it should be. The layout is flipped and there's not a single thing in here that feels *right*.

It's funny…I used to love my apartment. It was my favorite place in the world. A space that was all my own. Something just for me.

Now when I look around, I notice all the things that are missing.

Starting with *her*.

I sigh, scrubbing my hand through my hair and tugging on the ends in frustration. I am bored out of my fucking mind. The loneliness I haven't felt in the last month is kicking in.

I could call up Nolan and see if he wants to get a beer, but not even that sounds appealing. All he'll do the entire time is look at me with those *I told you so* eyes he's had trained my way since I moved out, and I'd rather not be reminded of what a mess this has become.

Leo's shell knocks against the glass of his terrarium, and I roll my head to the side to find him staring at me. He looks just as pitiful as me.

"I know, buddy. I miss her too."

How has it only been one week when it feels like a year?

I want to see her.

I *need* to see her.

I want to know why she wasn't there the morning I moved out. Why I woke up to a cold bed and haven't seen her since. Why she's been hiding in her apartment avoiding me when that doesn't sound anything like the promises we made.

I want to know why she didn't ask me to stay.

Why the hell did I want to stay?

I have to stop thinking about this. Have to stop thinking about her.

We said we'd go back to the way things were before. It was just sex, just relieving some tension.

No attachments.

I need to *un*attach myself from her.

I push myself up off the couch.

If she wants things to be normal between us, then back to normal they'll be.

Today is Sunday, and I should be at The Gravy Train getting some cherry pie.

It's exactly where I intend to be.

ALL WEEK I've felt like a bit of a circus sideshow.

Any time I run into someone else in the building, they stare or give me a sad smile, and any time I've walked into The Gravy Train, the same thing happens.

Like now.

I guess the news of me moving back into my apartment and River and I no longer spending time together has traveled fast through the busybodies.

I step in line to order my breakfast, Leo tucked safely to my side.

Usually when I bring him here, there are people clambering to see him.

Not today.

It's like I'm some sort of pariah and I don't understand why.

I peer around the old diner, and almost everyone who makes eye contact with me quickly looks away.

All right then. Weird.

Then, I see her.

And suddenly I don't see anything else.

She's by herself. A cup of coffee and bag of M&M'S I know she's spent too much time separating sit in front of her.

Her red hair, the sight of which makes my fingers tingle as I vividly recall the feeling of having it wrapped around my fist, is pulled into a tidy bun, a few tendrils hanging down around her face. Her plain white shirt stands out against the brightness of her hair and her burnt orange shorts. Her legs are crossed, the top one swinging back and forth with impatience as she waits on Maya and Sam.

Her fingers are busy pushing around the chocolate candies, and it's the sole focus of her concentration, so it takes her a while to notice my longing stare burning through her—but I know the second she does.

Goose bumps form across her skin, and she turns her head my way.

Even from across the diner, the hitch in her breath when our eyes collide is obvious.

I want to swallow that breath with my own because *fuck* I have missed her lips.

She sits up straighter on her stool, pushing her shoulders back and averting her gaze.

I smirk, moving forward in the line.

I guess that's where we're going with this.

"Hey, Darlene," I say with a smile when I reach the front counter.

She doesn't return my pleasantries. Instead, she sighs. "What'll it be, Dean?"

Okay...

"Just a slice of cherry and a coffee, please."

"We're out of cherry."

"Out?" I slide my gaze to the pie station, which obviously contains two full cherry pies. I point at them. "There's some right there."

"Like I said, we're out," she insists.

Ah. I see.

She's mad at me for what happened with River, even though nothing happened with her.

"Can I get the apple then?"

"Out."

"Pumpkin?"

"It's summer, kid. You know that's seasonal."

"What about blackberry?"

"You're in luck—we just so happen to have some."

Of course. Because that's River's least favorite kind.

I reach into my wallet to pay and peek over at her.

She's watching me with a satisfied grin on her face.

Brat.

"Darlene, did I, um, do something to upset you?"

Her eyes flit River's way. "No."

I sigh. "You know we didn't break up, right? We weren't dating. She was just letting me stay there. That's all."

Darlene pins me with a stare. "I wasn't born yesterday, Dean. I know you two had a thing and I know you left and moved back into your apartment." She points toward River. "I also know that girl hasn't been in here with a smile since *and* missed cherry pie day all last week." A shake of her head. "If you're going to go with the 'just roommates' bit, might want to make it more believable."

With that, she scurries off to grab my order.

I'm left standing there surprised.

River hasn't been in since I moved out?

That's…interesting.

And damn surprising.

Maybe my moving out had more effect on her than I thought.

"Thanks," I say to Darlene when she slides the pie and coffee across the counter. I toss her a big tip in her jar, just to make her feel bad for taking River's "side."

She grunts again, and I grab my slice, balancing my plate on Leo's hut with ease, something I've perfected over the last year.

I make my way over to River's table. Slip onto the stool across from her. Not to be an ass and screw with her, but because I *always* sit here on Sundays. Besides, it's a community table. I can sit where I please.

Lucy, who I didn't even notice before, is sitting in her usual corner. She snickers when I plop down, and I toss her a wink.

"Hey, Lucy."

Another laugh. "Dean."

I pull my plate off Leo's hut and work to get us situated.

"River," I say to her, reaching for a green M&M.

She slides them all away before I grab hold of one. "Ass."

She's not calling me one. She's using it as my name.

My lips twitch. "No Maya and Sam today?"

"Nope."

"How have you been?"

"Doing great," she snaps. "I'll be even better here soon."

"That so?"

"Yep. I—oh goodie! Here they are!"

She holds her hands out for the *two* full pies being thrust her way.

"Thanks, Darlene," she says. "You're the best."

"Anything for you, dear." She smiles sweetly at her, then shoots daggers my way before returning to her spot behind the counter.

River sets her pies on the table and pops the lid open on one of them. She grabs the fork I didn't even notice she had and stabs into it.

Right in the middle.

"That is just wrong on so many levels." I shake my head.

She ignores me as she shoves a forkful of warm cherry pie into her mouth, moaning dramatically around the utensil.

The sound goes straight to my cock, and it twitches with excitement.

Then she drags her tongue slowly over the silverware, making sure to get *every last crumb* off of it, and I have to spread my legs, needing the room in my jeans.

I swallow thickly, trying to get a hold of myself.

She gives me a mischievous smirk.

She fucking knows what she's doing to me.

It's been just over a week since I was inside her, and that's far too damn long for me, especially with her torturing me like she is.

"*Wow.* I think they might have put extra love in these today. This is amazing!"

Another bite. Another fucking moan.

I get it. It's payback. For all those times I "stole" her pie, even though I always technically bought her some.

But there's something else to it that feels...vindictive, especially because we're in public and I can't do anything about it.

It's like she's mad at me for leaving when she's the one who never asked me to stay.

Part of me wishes we were anywhere else right now so I could talk to her about it.

Another part of me knows being alone with River is only going to lead to one thing, and it's definitely not part of our "back to being neighbors" plan.

No attachments. Just neighbors.

Last I checked, most neighbors don't tongue-fuck a fork right in front of you.

Game on, River.

Chapter 21

RIVER

"HOLD IT!"

I know that voice.

I smash the *Close Door* elevator button over and over.

It's no use.

Dean's arm slides between the doors at the last minute, and he shoves them apart, wiggling inside.

"Hey, man"—he shakes his wet hair out—"I said hold it—"

His lips part when he sees it's me, surprised.

He recovers quickly, his tongue darting out to wet his lips.

I try to forget how good his tongue feels wetting other places.

"You." His eyes fall to slits as he hitches the soggy grocery sack he's holding up higher. "You pressed *Close Door*, didn't you?"

"Guilty." I grin. No sense in trying to deny it.

"It's raining sideways out there."

I shrug, and he turns toward the front of the elevator with an annoyed huff as the car begins its ascent.

Water droplets *plop, plop, plop* onto the floor.

Unable to help myself, I steal a glance at him out of the corner of my eye.

Even soaking wet, he looks good.

His black hair is a mess, that ever-present stubble along his jawline still there. Those long, muscular legs of his are clad in a pair of jeans that hug his ass way too well. He's sporting a Metallica t-shirt that's just wet enough and tight enough to give the imagination something to cling to.

Only I don't have to use my imagination.

I know exactly what's under that shirt.

Know how much he likes it when I pepper kisses down his stomach. How much it makes him squirm and curse when I run my tongue over the muscles he's worked so hard to build. And how it really drives him wild when I drag my fingernails across his skin when I'm on my knees for him.

His jaw twitches, and I know he's aware of me looking at him.

All of him.

Including the bulge that's steadily growing with each passing floor.

Is he thinking about it too?

You can hear the claps of thunder even inside the elevator, and I'm thankful they cover my stuttered breaths.

"How's Morris?" he asks, breaking the tension.

I know he's not truly asking about my cat. He abhors Morris.

"Better than he's ever been," I lie.

He grunts.

The power in the building surges and the elevator grinds to a sudden stop. I lose my balance, falling right into Dean, who drops his groceries in an effort to catch me.

It goes dark.

"Shit," he mutters, wrapping an arm around me and pulling me against him.

The power surges again, and we're rocked the other way.

My back is against the wall, one of Dean's arms around me, the other pressed against the ceiling above our heads.

The lights flicker back to life, and the elevator continues its ascent, but this time much, much slower.

We don't move, and we barely breathe.

His fingers flex on my waist as he drops his head, his lips finding a spot on my exposed shoulder. One soft kiss. Then another. And a third. All in a line, tracing up my neck while his fingers go the opposite direction.

He plays with the hem of my short cotton shorts, dipping his fingers dangerously close to places he's not supposed to be touching as he continues to kiss up my neck. There's no way he doesn't feel me clench my thighs together. No way he doesn't feel the heat coming from between them.

His lips are at my ear when the car dings, announcing its arrival on our floor.

His fingers dig into my thighs, and he curls his other hand into a fist that he taps against the wall once. Twice. Like he's fighting with himself.

Cold sweeps over me when he pulls away, peering down at me with glassy, lust-filled eyes.

"There," he says quietly, voice hoarse like he's the one dying. "Now we're both wet."

He grabs his things and disappears.

The doors close, and I take my first real breath in far too long.

IF YOU'D HAVE TOLD me over a month ago I'd be back here in my tub sipping on whiskey and eating pie, I'd have laughed.

But that's exactly what I'm doing.

I cut off a forkful of cherry pie and take a bite.

Imagine my surprise when it does nothing to satiate the hunger inside of me.

It's completely Dean's fault.

His antics in the elevator still have me out of whack hours later.

As soon as I regained my composure and made it into my apartment, I knew I needed to do something to take the edge off. I tried meditation. Yoga. Even tried masturbating, but it just wasn't the same as what Dean had done to me.

Nothing worked.

It doesn't help that I was so exhausted this morning when my alarm went off that I called in sick. That's twice in two weeks.

I blame Dean for that too.

It's hard to see him. To be around him. I'm trying to go on as we planned, like nothing happened. No making it awkward.

But the truth is, it's pure torture to have to see him.

The most maddening part of it all is that this suffering was mostly my idea. Sure, Dean was the one to suggest we relieve the building tension, but did I have to be so damn adamant about rules? Why did I ever think we could go back to the way things used to be after all was said and done?

I knew.

Knew there was a chance I'd fall for Dean. Even if it was minuscule at first, it was there.

Yet, I agreed to our arrangement.

I wanted a taste that bad.

Now I have to live with the consequences of falling for him.

Why the hell did I ever think this was a good idea?

Because Maya is right—you never hated him.

I didn't.

I don't.

But I wish I truly hated him. It would make all this a whole lot easier.

I abandon my pie and set the to-go container on the ledge, sinking lower into the bubbles, relishing the warmth of the water. I allow my eyes to fall shut, and those damn green orbs haunt me again.

They were there last night too. And the night before. And the one before that.

They're always there, staring at me in the otherwise dark void.

Dean's eyes.

Bright, beautiful, and inviting.

I miss them. Miss his warmth. His laugh. That smirk. Even him stealing all my groceries and fighting with Morris.

I miss *him*.

"STILL LIKE THAT OLD TIME ROCK 'N' ROLL!"

I yelp, jumping at the sudden sound. Water sloshes all over the bathroom, and I'm instantly annoyed.

I did *not* miss that.

"Dean!" I shout at the noise, even though he can't hear me.

I push up out of the tub, yank my towel from the rack, and stomp through the apartment.

Not today, Dean Evans. Not today.

I dry off quickly and this time have enough sense to at least wrap my robe around my form before swinging open my front door and going right over to his. I pound on the wood so hard I can hear stuff in my apartment rattle.

BANG! BANG! BANG!

"Dean!" I holler again. "Turn it down!"

A few seconds go by…and the volume increases.

"Oh, you have got to be kidding me." I growl, slapping the door again. "Dean Evans! Open this door right now or I swear I will—"

I stumble as the door is jerked open but recover quickly, jutting my chin out as he towers over me with playful eyes.

He leans against the doorjamb, crossing his arms. The muscles jump and pulse, and I try not to pay attention to them as I give him a scornful look.

"River. What brings you by?"

Chapter 22

DEAN

THERE IS something seriously wrong with me.

I knew touching her in the elevator was a bad idea.

But I knew not touching her was equally bad.

It took every ounce of strength I could muster to walk away, to just let her be. I've never had to fight myself so hard before.

River wants to go back to the way things were. She's been harping on it since I moved in.

If that's what she wants, I'll do it for her.

I twist the knob on my stereo, and the music fills the room.

I have no doubt it's too loud. In fact, I'm willing to bet she'll be pounding on my door in three...

Two...

One...

BANG! BANG! BANG!

I smile.

See? Something *is* wrong with me.

I can't help it though. I miss her. Want and will use any excuse to be around her. Even if it means she's just coming over here to yell, at least I'll get to see her again.

With slow steps, I make my way down the hall, letting her simmer out there before yanking it open.

She stumbles back but catches herself quickly. She pokes her chin out, pushing her tits up and meeting me head-on.

I smirk down at her, noting that this time she was at least smart enough to throw on a robe before traipsing over here.

"River. What brings you by?"

"Are we really going to have a repeat of this again? Last I checked, it didn't end too well for you."

Damn. I am never going to live that fire down, am I?

Never mind that.

I tip my head. "But it turned out well for you, didn't it?"

She knows exactly what I'm referring to—all the nights I spent in her bed, all the nights I made her scream and helped her find relief.

She rolls her eyes. "Yes, so what? I just love still living next door to you, especially now that you can torture me in the same ways you did before."

"Is that what I'm doing?" I lean down, too close because I can smell the flowery scent of bubble bath. "Torturing you?"

"Yes!" She throws her hands into the air, and I barely hold back my laugh.

She looks ridiculous right now. Hair haphazardly held together by a clip. Bright pink fuzzy robe wrapped around her. Bare feet and not a stitch of makeup on.

God, I want her.

"Don't pretend you don't know what you're doing, Dean. That stunt in the elevator wasn't cool."

"Just like it wasn't cool for you to practically tongue-fuck that fork at the diner yesterday. If you want to play silly games, I can play them too."

With a growl, she shoves at my chest, pushing me into my apartment.

I chuckle darkly. "What? Giving in so soon?"

"No!"

She slams the door closed, chasing me farther inside.

"What are you doing, Dean? You're driving me insane! We were supposed to go back to normal, not torture each other more."

I work my jaw back and forth, the frustration bubbling up as she reminds me of the rules yet again.

"Right, the rules." I snort. "Fuck the rules."

She jams an angry finger my way. "You agreed to them, Dean. You said it too. When your apartment was done, we were done. That was that."

"That was before I knew you were going to completely fucking own me!"

She stumbles back at my loud words.

My chest deflates, like a weight has been lifted off my shoulders, and it's suddenly obvious to me what was happening all along.

I was falling for her.

Oh shit.

I love her.

I am *in love* with River White.

I've *been* in love with her, probably longer than I care to admit. I've never hated her. I've just met her ire pound for pound because it was fun to mess with her.

I've always admired her, always looked forward to seeing her.

It's never been hate. We've never been enemies.

We're just idiots who can't see what's right in front of us.

"W-What?" She gapes up at me with wide eyes.

I exhale slowly and take a step toward her. Then another.

She gulps when we're standing just six inches apart.

"You own me, River."

"I… No. I don't."

I nod. "You do. You fucking do and it drives me mad that you do."

She peers up at me, eyes full of surprise and worry and confusion and so many of the same things I'm feeling.

"I don't know when it happened—maybe it's always been the case—but it's true. You're smart and funny. You challenge me every fucking second of every day, always keeping me on my toes. And you're drop-dead fucking gorgeous on top of it."

She scoffs. "Yes, so hot right now."

"Even right now, because you're so authentically you. Unapologetic about who you are and what you want."

"Please. I can hardly decide what I want for dinner most nights."

"Stop trying to talk me out of it."

She darts her tongue out, wetting her lips. Her eyes flit off to the side, looking anywhere but at me. "That's not what it was supposed to be," she says quietly.

I nod. "I know. But it just is what it is."

Her breaths are coming in sharper. "No labels."

Another step. "I know."

"No pressure."

Another, and we're so close I can see the swirls of color in her eyes. "I know."

"No attachments, Dean."

I slide my finger under her chin and tilt her face up. Her

bottom lip is captured between her teeth, and her eyes are full of so many emotions.

I give her a lazy grin. "Oops."

"You left," she whispers, dropping her forehead to my chin.

I press a kiss to the top of her head. "You didn't ask me to stay."

"I wanted to. I was scared. The rules…"

"Fuck the rules," I repeat.

Then I cup her face and claim her mouth.

I kiss her slowly. Softly.

I tell her I love her without using the words.

We're both gasping for air when I finally pull my lips from hers.

"This is a bad idea."

"Absolutely awful," I agree.

"We're neighbors. What if this doesn't work out? Then what happens? We already failed at trying to make things not be awkward and go back to the way they were before. How are we going to navigate after something real?"

"I think what we had was real."

"I'm being serious."

"So am I, but if you want an answer for it, how about this: if things go south between us, you can move."

She growls. "Dean…"

I laugh. "I'm kidding. Kind of." I lick my dry lips. "I doubt we'll have to worry about it not working out."

"Why do you say that?"

"Because we survived living together once when you truly hated me. We'll survive again."

She chews on her bottom lip, thinking it over.

Finally, she nods. "Okay."

"Okay?" I ask quietly, lightly brushing my mouth over hers.

"Okay, but I have to tell you something first."

"What?"

"I broke them too…the rules. I got attached."

I laugh. "No shit."

"I don't hate you, Dean."

"I know, River." I sigh against her lips. "I don't hate you either."

Epilogue

RIVER

"DEAN! SERIOUSLY!" I bang on his front door. "I am *so* over this!"

The music flips off, and he swings the door open, shirtless.

In nothing but a towel.

"What!"

I lift a brow at him, scrolling my eyes over his impeccable body. "You better not answer your door like that all the time."

"And if I do?"

"Then your girlfriend is going to be *big mad*."

He rolls his eyes. "At least be *big mad* in here."

He pulls me inside, letting the door slam closed behind him.

He crowds me up against the closest wall, his lips dropping to my neck. The stubble on his chin brushes against my skin, and it pebbles at the contact.

I can already feel his dick hardening.

We've been officially dating for three months now, and a simple touch from him still sets my body on fire.

It's hard to think there was a time when I ever hated him.

He still annoys me to no end, but it just means things will

always be interesting between us. He still steals my pie, but he still buys it too. And for all the times he's the worst neighbor ever, he makes up for it by being the best boyfriend ever.

I can't remember a time when I was happier.

"What are you banging on my door for anyway?" he mumbles against me.

"Your music was too loud."

"That would be your cat's fault."

"Morris? What did he do?"

He looks down at me, brows drawn tight. "Little shithead found his way inside my apartment. He snuck all the way to the bathroom and knocked my speaker off the counter. I had to improvise for my after-gym shower."

"Remind me to thank him."

"He ruined my speaker—my *expensive* speaker. We aren't thanking him. This is like the third thing he's knocked off my counters in the last few months. That doesn't even include all the times he's snuck over here before to terrorize me." He gapes. "Do you have him *trained* to torture me, River?"

I laugh. "No, but that's not a bad idea."

He shakes his head. "This is exactly why I have Leo. He's quiet, doesn't smart back to me, and doesn't ruin my shit. I vote we trade Morris in for another turtle."

I gasp. "No way!"

"Worth a shot." He shrugs. "You know…there is a way for us to avoid your cat sneaking over to my apartment."

"You learn to close your door and I'll learn to close mine?"

He grins down at me. "Or I move in."

"With…me?"

He nods slowly, eyes tentative.

Nervous.

This moment is one of the few times I've seen Dean be vulnerable and not his usual cocky self.

"You want to move in with me?" I repeat.

"Yes. Unless you'd rather move in with me."

"Are you serious?"

"Yes."

Dean wants to live together. That's huge.

But truth be told, I've been thinking about it for some time.

After we officially got together, we decided we'd live apart. We didn't want to put any extra pressure on our relationship, and all the reasons we had for doing it made sense at the time.

Now, I can't seem to think of a single reason for us *not* to live together.

He shrugs. "Why not? I mean, is the suggestion all that surprising? Last I checked, we're dating now. Have been for a while. It wouldn't be completely insane for us to take that next step." He brushes his lips against mine. "Besides, think of all the ways we could use our extra time together."

A slow grin pulls at my lips when he uses a variation of the same speech he gave when he proposed our *just sex* arrangement. "Did you really just use that same speech on me again?"

"Depends. Did it work again?"

"Do you not remember what happened last time I fell for it?"

"Quite clearly. And I don't know about you, but I'm pretty happy with the results."

"I am too."

His grin widens. "So, what do you say? Want to give the roommates thing a shot again?"

"Hmm…" I tap my chin. "I guess it's not the worst idea you've ever had."

"Gonna need a clear answer on this one, River."

I laugh. "Yes, I—"

Just like the first time we dove headfirst into a crazy agreement, he kisses me.

Just like the first time, my heart goes wild.

And it's safe to say I don't hate Dean Evans at all.

Other Titles by Teagan Hunter

CAROLINA COMETS

Puck Shy

ROOMMATE ROMPS SERIES

Loathe Thy Neighbor

Love Thy Neighbor

Crave Thy Neighbor

Tempt Thy Neighbor

SLICE SERIES

A Pizza My Heart

I Knead You Tonight

Doughn't Let Me Go

A Slice of Love

Cheesy on the Eyes

TEXTING SERIES

Let's Get Textual

I Wanna Text You Up

Can't Text This

Text Me Baby One More Time

INTERCONNECTED STANDALONES

We Are the Stars

If You Say So

HERE'S TO SERIES

Here's to Tomorrow

Here's to Yesterday

Here's to Forever: A Novella

Here's to Now

Want to be part of a fun reader group, gain access to exclusive content and giveaways, and get to know me more?

Join Teagan's Tidbits on Facebook!

Want to stay on top of my new releases?

Sign up for my newsletter at

www.teaganhunterwrites.com/newsletter

Acknowledgments

Dean Winchester, thanks for being an inspiration for my Dean.

My Marine, because every day I wake up thinking, *I'm hungry*. And you feed me. Thank you.

Mom, I love you.

Laurie, I think this is the first year we've gone since we met without seeing each other. It feels *really* weird. I can't wait to hug you again. Thank you for being my rock and the working half of my brain.

My #soulmate, if there's anyone in this world that I know I could call and talk to about anything and everything, even 2,000 plus miles away, you're that person. I love you.

Caitlin, I truly cannot imagine writing a book without you. Thank you for your patience, your guidance, and your cheerleading. I owe so much to you.

Julie Griffis and Judy, thank you for being my third and fourth set of eyes!

Tidbits, thank you for always being there when I need a laugh. And for standing by when I need a break. Your support...it drives me so much more than you could ever know.

And finally...to you, Reader. Writing a book during a pandemic is really weird. Especially writing romance where it's all sunshine and rainbows. This book was hard to write for so many reasons, but not one of them was my lack of love for Dean and River, and I hope you could feel that. Thanks for taking the chance on my new Roommate Romps Series! I hope you're ready to laugh!

With love and unwavering gratitude,
    Teagan

About the Author

TEAGAN HUNTER is a Missouri-raised gal, but currently lives in South Carolina with her Marine veteran husband, where she spends her days begging him for a cat. She survives off coffee, pizza, and sarcasm. When she's not writing, you can find her binge-watching various TV shows such as *Supernatural* and *One Tree Hill*. She enjoys cold weather, buys more paperbacks than she'll ever read, and never says no to brownies.

www.teaganhunterwrites.com

Printed in Great Britain
by Amazon

82572716R00150